THE UNPROPOSED Guy

Bhavik Sarkhedi

&

Suhana Bhambhani

Leadstart
INKSTATE

ISBN: 978-93-5610-724-3

First published in India 2022 by Leadstart Inkstate
A brand of One Point Six Technologies Pvt. Ltd.

123, Building J2, Shram Seva Premises,
Wadala Truck Terminal,
Mumbai 400022, Maharashtra, INDIA
Phone: +91 96999 33000
Email: info@leadstartcorp.com
www.leadstartcorp.com

Disclaimer: This is a work of fiction. All the names, characters, businesses, places, events and incidents in this book are either the product of the author's imagination or used in a fictitious manner. Any resemblance to actual persons, living or dead, or actual events is purely coincidental.

Editor: Kavya Shree
Cover: Komal Kohok
Layouts: Kevis Tech

Contents

About the Authors

BHAVIK SARKHEDI is the published author of 3 books including *The Weak Point Dealer* and *Will You Walk a Mile?* He is an ambivert who likes to explore the intersection of human psychology and life's philosophy. He is the only Indian writer who has made it to Google's 'best content writers on the world' list. He is also the founder of multiple content writing service agencies that deliver quality content. With his parent organization Write Right and its subsidiaries Estorytellers, Taletel and Kalam Kagaz, Bhavik is changing the Indian content writing industry, literally, one word at a time. This young entrepreneur has become an inspiration for passionate writers and authors trying to make their mark in the content writing space.

SUHANA BHAMBHANI is a former investment banker with an eminent zeal for writing. She gives her best writing in creative content and article scripting. She has delivered inventive content specialising in ghostwriting. Mother of a four-year-old boy, she balances her personal as well as professional commitments passionately. *The Unproposed Guy* is Suhana's debut novel.

Acknowledgements

Bhavik

This book wouldn't be possible without Suhana as she gave this concept a staunch foundation of the creative imagination we had. *The Unproposed Guy* wouldn't become a reality without the support of my wife Darshana and my parents.

Suhana

Firstly, I would like to thank my co-author Bhavik Sarkhedi for helping me bring my dream to reality. I could not have done this without his support and passion for networking. His motivating nature and high experience in the field enthused me to follow my aspiration and pen down my scripting into my first official book.

I would also like to thank my husband and my family who have been a constant pillar of strength, making the harmony of personal and penning obligations a success for me. It only made both my journey and its aim substantially worthwhile.

Authors' Note

Dear Readers,

Welcome to the life of Kevin! It is filled with fun, laughter, drama, and many romances—correction, failed romances. As you hop onto his rollercoaster life, also take a dive into some "Feats of Kevin", as we would like to call his stellar performances. Hope you have a good ride!

1

The Groom

"I do look good. Maybe…okay?" As his reflection shone in the mirror, Kevin murmured to himself. It was a big day for him as he was getting married. He took in a gulp of air and breathed out.

The early May sun peeked out of the white clouds. A pleasant breeze from the north rustled in through the window as sweet strains of wedding music drifted across the venue.

I can't believe it, I am finally getting married!

"Kevin, where are you lost? It's your wedding day!" His sister's voice floated in from somewhere nearby, already well aware of his state of mind.

"Kevin, are you ready?" She called out again.

"Yes, Tina. I am almost ready." Kevin shook his arms in an attempt to push all thoughts out of his head.

As she stepped into the room of the groom, Tina looked at him happily.

"I am so happy for you. Oh brother, you are finally getting married! I have to ask, are you excited? You must be…right?" A hint of concern apparent in that last word.

"Um…"

Tina wondered if now was the perfect time she made sure Kevin knew of her further intentions.

Before he could say anything, she quickly said with affirmation, "Once you are off the hook, I can finally start planning my wedding with my dream groom, my prince charming." Looking at him top to toe, she grinned.

"This 'tie the knot' sort of appearance on you makes you look so different, weird too." She chuckled at Kevin.

"Relax, sister!" Kevin sighed deeply. He already knew as this day would come, Tina would have made her future plans as well. He knew his sister well and loved her no matter what. Her happiness made him content.

"Okay. You get ready; I will check on mummy and papa in the meanwhile."

"Yeah." Kevin knew it was his day, and he was nervous.

He looked in the mirror again as he adjusted his hair, thinking that he looked odd, almost like having the legendary Captain Jack Sparrow at a formal cocktail party.

"Like the captain said, 'Close your eyes and pretend it's all a bad dream. That's how I get by.'" He muttered out loud.

2

The Friends

"Hey Kevin, how are you, bro?"

As Kevin's buddies entered the room, he felt butterflies in his stomach. They were his strength and weakness. They knew him in and out. He had lived his journey of friendship with their love, fights and thrilling experiences. Dev, Kabir and Ansh were a huge part of his life.

"I am okay, Dev."

"Your day has come. Get ready to be enslaved by your partner!"

"You know, just like us." Ansh quipped.

"Guys, guys. Can you stop goofing and help me with my sherwani here?"

"Yeah, hold your patience, Kevin. We know you are getting married today!"

"Chill, Kabir!"

"Being so impatient doesn't suit you, Kevin. Especially for your first night. Your night of love!" Everyone except Kevin—who looked slightly uncomfortable—roared with laughter.

Kevin and his friends shared a close bond and he knew they had a playful streak in them.

"Keep in mind my golden words. The words of Ansh: Marriage is like a video game…"

"Is it?" Dev asked, quirking a brow.

"Maybe for you." Kabir butted in.

"Guys, let me finish!" Ansh raised his voice. "Marriage is like a video game…starts off easy, then gets harder, and eventually you go online and find a way to escape."

"True. Bravo. Hardcore." The other two chorused while Kevin looked at them amused.

"Here, we got you a first-night gift too. Your very own, glow in the dark…wait for it…"

"Boxer shorts!" They screamed gleefully.

Kevin's face turned pink. "Guys, glow in the dark?"

"Yes. For you to have some fun."

"Oh, don't worry, these shorts are incredibly comfortable and feature a lit-up bulb with a glowing 'turned on' sign when the lights are completely off." Ansh explained, trying to be helpful.

"Bro, you seem ready! Let's get you married!" His friends wished the best for him. They wanted him to have a happy married life just like all of them.

"Come on, guys, let's all go down to the mandap. Kevin, your brother Zubin has arranged for some wedding events too. Let's go!" Kevin followed them quietly, unsure what to expect.

3

The Family

"Here is your watch. Listen, do I look good in this saree?"

"You look great. Who would say you are the groom's mother?"

"Ahh, let it be. You do look like the groom's father, though."

Kevin's parents, like most Indian parents, had conservative beliefs, certain restrictions towards modern norms and some favouritism between their children.

"I am sure Kevin won't be ready. He has no value for time. Look at my Zubin, he is so responsible. He is already dressed and is even taking care of getting the work here done faster. The caterers, the decorations, the band…he has handled it all. Alone. That's my Zubin." Zubin, their first born was the favoured child of the house and the parents' dearest.

"Yes, your Zubin is excellent."

"My Zubin? Is he not your son?"

"Yes. But it is Kevin's day today." Kevin's mother said, feeling a hint of guilt.

"Even Tina is looking gorgeous." His father commented as if Kevin was of no importance in his world.

"Indeed."

"Are you ready?"

"Let's get going. We need to take care of many rituals at hand."

A big gate, heavy with decoration, was ready. All special arrangements for food were in the adjoining shamiana. Confectioners set to work, preparing excellent dishes for serving. The entrance was beautifully lit with electric bulbs and sparkling lights. The band was playing. And a white decorated mare stood at the gate, ready to serve its duty as the groom's ride for the day. The photographers were clicking the crowd passionately in an effort to get as many good photos as they could.

"Kevin! Good you have come down finally. Have a look at your stage. I, your superhero brother, arranged it all. Looks great, right?" Zubin was exhilarated. Maybe not because his brother was finally getting married but more so as he would get to solely arrange, decide and plan the things which made him feel like the leader of the family.

With a thin-lipped smile, Kevin said, "Yeah. It looks good, Zubin."

"Right. So how is the feeling inside?" He tapped Kevin's chest.

"I am alright!" Though he was a bundle of nerves, he did not feel the need to share any of it with his brother.

"Super! The photographer needs you for some shots. Go now to the selfie corner." Zubin turned him in the right direction and gave him a little push.

"Okay." Kevin knew he had to listen to his elder brother. This was their relationship, even when they were kids and even today, his big day, his wedding day.

4

The Wedding Shenanigans

"Hi, Kevin. Congratulations! I am your official wedding photographer. We need to take a few solo pictures of you first."

Kevin was ready to take his official wedding pictures. Though he felt pretty awkward as he never believed in posing or taking a selfie; he disliked posing. For him, pictures made real memories and not just reel fun.

"Come here. Now smile."

The photographer yelled a myriad of instructions at him:

"Stand here. Now look there."

"Pose like this."

"Yeah. Now, give me a 'wisdom wala' look."

"Good. Now, show that YOU ARE SUPER HAPPY!"

"Come on, Kevin, I need decent pictures for today. I don't want just any shutterbug snapping."

"You have to give me timeless treasures that I can share even with your future generations. Don't forget that!"

"Okay." Though Kevin was still trying to pose for his wedding day pictures, all he could think of was when will it get over and he could be with the one he loved, forever.

Getting Married was painted across the banner behind him. The place was teeming with guests. Kevin's cousins were pouting away for that perfect selfie. Balloons and decorations fluttered around the railing and banisters, a festive mixture of red, light blue, and golden. The women were showing off their jewellery and attire to each other, trying to make the other one jealous, while the children ran around and danced. Everywhere one looked, it was bright, colourful and grand.

"Kevin, come with us." His buddies called. "As it is, you will not have much time for your buds anymore."

"Have a sip; it's your favourite." Dev said, handing him a Mojito.

"Thanks, guys. I needed this," Kevin responded after relishing few sips without pausing.

"We know. Every guy requires the strength to trade his bachelorhood away this day." Ansh retorted.

"You can taste some food too. You do seem hungry. It is a variety of delicious food, Kevin." Kabir looked concerned for his friend.

"Huh." The last thing he needed was food but he couldn't tell them that.

"You will see all your guests can be seen at the food counter itself."

"See Sharma Uncle, not leaving the pani poori counter. Poor Savita Aunty, she looks tired waiting in line behind him." One of his friends pointed out and Kevin's gaze followed, focusing on faces he knew while some he could not remember ever coming across.

But the air was filled with laughter in that moment, and that's all mattered.

Kevin's Feats

Who is Kevin?

He drinks green tea, not just espresso,

He likes all kinds of music, not just Despacito.

He is funny, but he fails to show it to his girl,

She gets sweet gifts, but he just can't buy her a pearl,

He loves it when in the gown he bought, she makes a twirl.

Like everyone, he too needs a partner,

Unlike anyone, he wishes to be her armour.

Thought he was a charmer, sharper and smarter,

Unfortunately, for her he becomes like a kindergartner.

He drives her crazy in long rides, being himself with her,

Nonetheless, she just considers him as her chauffeur.

He is not rude; he is straightforward,

Nevertheless, she thinks he makes it awkward.

She has many friends in guys; he is insecure,

So to get her attention, he skips his supper.

Her touch is ecstatic for him, he feels,

Her smile makes his whole day, he's head over heels.

Every time she calls on him, he drops what he does,

He wasn't her best bud, but that wasn't the fuzz.

She can't be his friend, he thinks and reels,

Before he is friend-zoned, he goes on and kneels.

He proposes to her and she treats it as fun,

Like every other, she says, 'You are not the one,'

It was all over again when it was time to run.

He thought all his life, he stood by her side.

But she just considered him Romeo who always lied.

He felt out of pride and the high tide rose inside.

Why is it so that his rhyme has to be perfect and his delivery flawless?

Why is it that the burden is always on him who can't seek solace?

Why is it so that he is devoid of love and care and becomes clueless?

He may not be Chandler Bing, but he has a good sense of humour,

He may not be Sheldon Cooper, but he has no brain tumour.

He may not be your fictional character, but he is a real funny narrator,

To all the ones who think 'I lack that Proposed-Factor,'

You don't lack anything because you are a New-clear reactor.

He may not be proposed anytime because he ain't desperate every time.

How does Kevin feel?

They say that the journey is more important than the destination,

But those who have to walk alone, seldom see the beauty in long roads.

Not having someone by your side dulls the colour,

How will someone on their own understand true beauty?

You always need glasses with love as a filter to understand it.

But how can I see it when even I do not know what it is?

Standing alone in a crowd and standing out is the only option for those who are not lonely otherwise.

A person who always stood alone wouldn't understand the hype of standing out from the crowd, but you have someone by your side that's why your voice is loud.

Why will someone who has nothing to fight for ever shout?

But when you have someone all along to hold your hand, whisper sweet nothings and tell you to stand ten feet tall,

Space is just a term for those who have someone to stay away from.

But what is it for a guy who stays alone all time; what does space really mean?

There's always some word which will never make sense to someone like us, who never know what being together means.

We will always be indifferent to some feelings and emotions as we never felt them.

Walking hand in hand with someone and smiling all the way along with them, and then hating them after that, arguing over nothing all day long and to be back to being happy again,

How are we supposed to understand that when we never experienced it?

They say men grow from their experiences.

So how can we grow without knowing that feeling?

And staying alone all the way long.

Those who have things often mistreat them and throw them out,

So what's wrong if someone else picks it up and treats it as a treasure?

For someone who stayed single all his life, relationship is a labyrinth,

One which each one of us wishes to get close to but never enters.

And they ask, what's the dilemma about falling in love?

Ask someone who has never or was never loved.

It's frightening to know the hands which you are holding right now might let you go,

It's comforting to sleep at night alone rather than having someone who will leave you all by yourself in that space you shared.

It's never the journey that is important for someone who has always been single.

It's always the destination.

The sooner we reach it,
The sooner it all ends.

Well, living alone is better than being left to live alone.

It's better to be never loved than craving for it after tasting it.

And then you ask, 'What's the dilemma of someone who has never been loved?'

Kevin's first performance in front of his friends

(The room echoed with laughter)

"See Kevin. We, your best buds, we care for you so much."

"We all love you, Kevin!" Kevin's friends hooted.

Awkward. Yeah, that could be the best word to describe the product of emotional reactions inside my body when I tried to flirt for the first time.

I am not even sure if that was flirting,

Just do not call it a cheap trick or I will be hurt!

Just kidding, I was a kid back then, not now, but still, don't!

So, coming back to the topic, MFF aka My First Flirt.

Fourteen I was back then, innocent fourteen, the age when the only Sunny I knew was Deol.

So, the girl I was talking about, Prachi was her name... Do not worry, we can use her name here because we never got a chance to talk after school; I am sure she does not even remember me now.

(Antaratma talking: "You did get a chance to talk to her after school you insecure, shy, and hopelessly awkward piece of shit!")

Sweet girl, but no one could actually defeat her when it came to arguments; she was a badass in her own way.

She was fierce, I remember her slapping a girl in front of the whole classroom, apparently for some stupid reason but who cares about the reasons, right? When in love, you don't have to know the real person to love her. Just kidding, my frustration for this hook-up culture kicked in, I guess.

Okay I should focus or we will never reach the main issue here.

So we were fourteen, I guess, I doubt if she even knew who I was.

Even if she did, she apparently had no reasons to ever call my name. 'The Unpopular Guy' that I was.

So all the students of my class were rebelling by playing together, girls and boys—our school had a strict "Stay the fuck away from girls" and vice versa policy.

Just to give you a vivid idea, one of the boys waved hello to a peer girl and she must have replied with a hello, which is a common guess people make, but the girl didn't reply. I mean, she did (complained to be exact), but to the wrong person (our class teacher), she was stupid.

Both the girl and the teacher, so it does not matter whom you consider stupid.

So in that environment we were rebelling and playing at the same time.

Sankal (chain) we called it (mera chain vain sub ujda... song running in the back of my head/ need to meditate/ I can rhyme well/ like if you threw me a grenade/ I will eat it like a cupcake...)

So, in this game one boy must touch another while running, gets to touch a girl if he is lucky!

I am not a pervert but that was the only physical contact I had with the opposite sex at that time, and also for a long time after that, poor me, ugh.

And the one you touch will then hold your hand and run with you, forming a chain (mera chain vai... Shut up, I definitely need to meditate!).

So, what happens is I somehow manage to touch her; I was faster than her in the game, so I got to touch her!

Now comes the best part, she was holding hands with me, like skin to skin contact you know, no gloves, no Corona.

My belly was dancing, the butterflies, those sensations, AYE HAYE...

We were running as they run in Bollywood movies, but I was not satisfied. I wanted more, so I took the step, the step of bravery.

As she was beside me, I played the card of a bug in the eye. I suddenly stopped and started acting as if a bug had entered my eye, my left eye to be exact so that when she would come close to look at the eye, our hearts could hear each other.

Yeah that was lame but I was not to blame because I was fourteen.

My plan worked, she stopped, and with her extremely caring eyes she started to inquire about me.

What happened?

I was dumbstruck, she was looking directly into my eyes; those butterflies evolved into DINOflies. She came closer to my eye with one hand stretched to see my retina better and blew a little air in there.

If I were a bug I would never come out like that, but there was no bug in there, the only bugs were my school friends, currently sitting backstage, looking at me.

One shouted "OH, MY BOY!"

That son of a bitch spoiled the moment and with him, all the other bugs started hooting at us on the playground.

It became too awkward for me, for us, for our sweet little love and the girl ran away, blushing, just to never even look at me again.

I was there alone, awkward, with no clue of what to do. But as usual, I was lost in the crowd, they forgot my name, but the story remained.

A small poem for those who still love the 90s

Be a child with your parents,

Be a dumbass with your friends,

Be mature with your colleagues,

Be a combination of all with your partner.

Some miscellaneous before I start my laughably boring ride:

Whatsapp = Where Thumbs up is the worst

Facebook = Where Thumbs up is used occasionally, frequently and forcefully

Tinder = Where Middle Finger is used literally after virtual Thumbs up

Metup = Failed Tinder

Happn = It never happens in India

Paytm ka Almamater = Cashback

Instagram = I want to be with/like Snapchat

Snapchat = I am taken

Twitter = I am committed to 140 characters

Reddit = I am the origin of everything on the Internet

Quora = I think I am Reddit for Indians

Wikipedia = Sadly, I am slowly turning into Quora

Tumblr = Who am I? What's the fuzz?

Pinterest = I am everywhere in Google Images after Imgur

Playstore = Kind of a 'free' store

iTunes = Not so kind and free

FM = I still exist

Calculator = When you can't add 10+10

Kevin on the Stage

> *Your mom just told you an awkward but hilarious joke and you're not sure if it's the joke that's funny or your mom telling the joke, but it doesn't matter, because now you're rolling on the floor and want to get up but you can't because your mom really caught you off-guard with the joke. You've been laughing for so long, your eyes start to water and the more you laugh, the funnier the joke seems.*
>
> *You're at your boring college graduation and it's time to issue the certificates. The principal gets up to issue the first set of awards. As she begins to walk with such gaiety and suaveness, smiling and intermittently posing for the camera, a lizard drops from the ceiling and onto her shoulders. She screams, cries, and jumps until her wig falls off. Everyone begins to laugh nonstop.*
>
> *All this is called humour. Humour has long been part of our lives—we see it when we watch an advertisement, a YouTube video, your favourite movie, an Instagram or twitter meme, or just sitting in the living room with your family. The effects of humour are also very beneficial and rewarding, but before I speak about the benefits, let's delve into its origin and the real meaning.*

Humour is simply any act, word, or phrase that causes laughter or evokes a feeling of pleasure in an individual. It creates a light-hearted atmosphere. The word 'humour' was derived from the Latin word for 'liquid' or 'fluid'. The ancient Greeks used this simple word to refer to the four main substances found throughout our bodies: yellow bile, black bile, blood and phlegm. Each of these bodily fluids were thought to influence our personality traits or overall character, as stated by Mayer (2019). Humour comes in many forms, shapes, colours and even odours—from the memes that we all love, to those silly jokes that we sometimes create, to impress that cute guy or girl or to just lessen the tension in a room.

Humour is used by almost everyone—well anyone who's not conceited and mundane—and reduces tension, anxiety and anger. Remember that time when you were upset over a situation and then your mom or dad gave you that encouraging speech with that sweet little joke at the end? Remember how less sad and more hopeful you eventually became? Well, that's one of the many powers of humour, it creates a feeling of happiness, hopefulness and joyfulness, which can later increase your confidence and self-esteem

So, what does being unproposed have to do with humour?

In a broad way, a sense of humour is connected and linked with context. You can't randomly crack jokes and make others laugh. The Unproposed Guy, with time, has realized it is the timing that matters more than the time.

Propose your brain with jokes and sarcasm; don't forget the context.

Humour also makes us more attractive and amiable. No one likes a frowning, unfriendly and unattractive being. Remember telling your best friend that 'he has a good sense of humour' or telling one of your boys that 'she's kinda funny'? That's the power of humour; it draws and connects people together.

So, what about your health?

Humour is not only great for your mental health, but it also improves your immune system by activating the immune cells and antibodies which fight infections. This enhances our resistance to diseases. When you laugh, your body releases a special chemical—endorphin—which reduces pain and increases pleasure. This also reduces stress and improves your mood.

Humour has so many great benefits yet we sometimes overlook it, but now that you're aware, spread the word and laugh your teeth out, well, I hope you have enough.

So, share a joke, laugh even if there's no joke (or if the joke you told isn't that funny), it'll be awkward, but rewarding.

The Unproposed Guy has been on a break for a long time but he has come to save the world from bad jokes, Covid-19, unemployment... but wait, is he employed?

Unproposed humour is akin to a failed attempt at making people laugh if you're a comedian, a witty speaker or a charming orator. But to be fair these are the only situations or bits which can tell you whether the Unproposed can one day be proposed, whether nonsenscial humour can one day become 'Oh, that makes so much sense' humour.

Amen!

Kevin friendship and bonding with the stage

People were grooving, ladies sweating out their cosmetic fine-tuning and gentlemen sweating out deodorants, while Florida's Club Can't Handle Me blasted through the speakers as I stood rooted, unable to handle her beauty.

Corona in one hand and a Dunhill in the other, she flaunted her perfect curves in her red attire, provoking me to feel jealous for not being in that dress. I know I'm being a perv, but two tequilas down already and a Carlsberg in hand, my mind was taking its own wild course.

The kohl enhanced her eyes, concealing those dark circles from her untimely stress or those late-night social media surfs. She gave me a friendly glance, but oh wait, did she just show me her prettiest curve? Should I go ask her to have a coffee with me?

Oh wait! I am in a pub, I can buy her a beer and be blessed again with that smile! Or am I too sloshed to be decent to a girl? Maybe I can ask her for a dance? No. A walk. Fuck, I am high.

Okay, let me just walk to her. It took me 20 long mins of deep thinking, a pint of beer, and three more crucial mins to walk to her with a heart full of planning of long drives, coffee dates, flirts, fucks and things which will lead me to a fruitful life with this beautiful lady!

But guess whom I got introduced to? Her girlfriend.

Is Kevin enjoying the stage

I had planned the whole conversation, from my How you doing to You can call me around 10 tonight! I was all set to be a chick magnet.

It was a cafe like the one where struggling writers hang around thinking of ideas, and I was no different. But today a rare sight caught my eye, and I couldn't resist it, thus, with all of the extroversion I had, I pushed myself to talk to that girl sitting at my 3 o'clock. Suppressing my anxiety, I walked up to her and uttered the magical words!

Which is supposed to get you the girl, like in an instant, according to Joey's philosophy. You watch Friends, right?

"How you doin'?"

The girl looked at me with her cat-like eyes & said, "EXCUSE ME?"

Excuse me? This wasn't supposed to be a part of the conversation! I hadn't thought about it... I thought she would say something like: "Am good...am good..."

I panicked as always. "That's a cool book you are reading!" (Girls like book talk, right?)

With a creepy smile on my face, I waited for her reply.

"Ohhh this book? Haven't you read it?"

"It looks like I have but I'm not sure." Me being me.

"You must be here for the first time then," she said.

"I'm…what?"

"Idiot, it's the cafe's menu!" And she burst into laughter.

"Ohkay. Am I…?" Again, me being me, "Utterly blunt!"

"Sit down, stupid!"

"So, you are among those hyper socially awkward boys who don't know how to talk to a girl?"

"Who the hell are you, calling me 'socially awkward' bitch?" my alter-ego spoke inside my head but she is cute, right? Right! My other side replied inside, and the usual numbness was on my facial display.

"So, you are. Just relax a little bit." As if those words ever relaxed me, my instincts uttered.

"You said something?" she asked, acting like she didn't hear me.

"Nope, nothing." Every cell inside my body was regretting my decision to make a move.

"Joey does not suit you, why don't you try more of a Chandler?" she stated.

"So, you do watch Friends!" I said with utmost delight.

"Yes, I love it, and he looks like you too…" she said.

And all of a sudden, my anxiety went away and I could be myself there.

And then we talked about Friends and books (not the menu card), movies, and some intellectual stuff for an hour or so, and I was convinced that tonight instead of Siri I would be talking to a real girl. As my date came to an end, I asked her for her number, and guess what? I got it. Smooth, right? I was more than happy.

But then I picked up on something, a tiny little flashy round hollow fucking engagement ring.

"That's a beautiful ring," I said.

"Thank you, and btw, you have to come to my wedding next month," she said like she fucking didn't know that that hollow metal pierced me.

"Sure," I said, and then she left. I finished my coffee and turned to my phone and said, "Hey, Siri, how you doin'?"

Round 2

Angel Priya is a fake name used by spammers to manipulate people. Tinder...yup I too had a tinder account. Unlike my real-life social image, I put a decent amount of time on my tinder status (poor old me!).

A selfie with my dog. "Men with dogs tend to attract women" is what I had heard. Another one with my guitar, for the same reason (I researched).

Tinder bio, that was the most exciting part. It felt like I was putting up my life's achievements (none at that time though, crying in the corner) in those two freaking lines. I tried my best and at the height of my creativity I came up with this: "I had a six-pack but donated five of them to charity." Lame, right? But that is the beauty of Tinder, no one can judge you until you slap them. Right? Behold the power of my swipes, bitches!

I was ready now. Two super sexy selfies and a great bio later, I was ready to be the Justin Bieber of Tinder, with regards to fame, of course (I was already a Justin Bieber in real-life when it came to singing; my father used to leave the house every time I started singing...).

I was going to pick the one I wanted to date, a superpower all men would trade their asses for! I had it, at least that is what I believed initially, swiping only the hottest ones on my first night, like those in a bikini looking like an hourglass… I remember laughing over a girl's profile, she was not even 19 at that time (nor was I, but you only judge others, right?) someone named ANGEL PRIYA with the cheesiest bio ever (Papa ki pari, main to udd chali). We all know a few of them, and then I slept, waiting for my fame to ascend overnight.

Good morning! I woke up, hopeful and restless just to check the matches; I was sure to hit a diamond that day, but zero! No matches at all, I was distressed. I left my bed to have coffee, black just because the milkman was on leave that day. Normally I would not mind a black coffee but that day, that freaking day, when I looked at the coffee, I swear, I could hear the liquid say, "I may be dark, but your dating future is darker," and that broke my spirit. I was just about to give up, but then I remembered, "Success does not happen overnight." That was enough to restore my confidence that day, and the day after and the day after… It lasted for a week, my pride was obliterated. A frustrated me started swiping right, in the night, at the speed of light! (Just showing off my rhyming skills!)

Good morning again, this morning was a little different because your man got a match (laughing like a devil inside). The notification had popped on my phone screen. 0.32 seconds, yup that's how long it took me to turn the app on. I had the smile of a grim reaper, the moment I checked who was the lucky girl!

You have a match: Angel Priya! And just like that my dating future went dark again.

Last Round (just wrapping this set up! It's worth it, I swear!)

I saw this wonderful girl when I was attending a blogging conference held in my city. I was obviously not expecting any diva to show up at a literature type event, but my anticipation proved right when she entered the room, and I said, "Oh my god, my conference is ruined. How will I be able to concentrate now?"

It was justified. I had to do something, something macho. What I did? By some crooked means, I found her email ID and sent the following:

"Hope this email finds you well. You must be in the pink of your health.

Duh, so formal. Yea, leave it.

Scene 1- You enter supposedly. Had I known I would craft an email for

it later, after struggling on Facebook, Instagram and probably Snapchat, I would

definitely have observed you better. Wait. What sort of

permutation and combination, had I applied? I mustn't tell you.

Scene 2- This was the adrenaline rush. So, today is the right time.

Maybe, tomorrow the gist and zeal might have faded, well, sort of, because of my impotency to pursue it personally.

Scene 3- Why would you come to the play today? You weren't there yesterday, for God's sake. If there was a test to 'being noticed' by someone with the most intellectually dumb patterns, I would be the winner and runner-up. Forgive my oxymorons.

Do you live in Ahmadabad? It's the only thing I probably don't know about you.

Anyway, I am going to be judged. Seriously, call it a one-day desperation or a new form of it, maybe 20–20, I just wanted to talk to you but couldn't.

See you. Needless to say, a sweet name you have.

PS.: Sonder = The realization that each random passer-by is living a life

as vivid and complex as your own."

The girl did get flattered but she refused to go out with me.

I am not Chandler Bing, but I have a good sense of humour

I don't look like Barney Stinson, but I am great with pickup lines

I am not Charlie Harper, but I am a decent guy with enough money

I am not Sheldon Cooper, but I am intellectual enough

I am not a Smurf, but I turn blues and reds often

I am not Michael Scofield, but I have many escape plans for life

I am not Theodral Bagwell, but I can be a badass whenever required

I am not Joey Tribbiani, but I am good at asking people how they are doing

I can't dance as good as MJ, but I have some sensational silly steps prepared for my girl

I am not Walter White, but I too have my own unfulfilled dreams

I am not Jesse Pinkman, but I drink and get high when I am happy

I am not Ross Geller, but I have soft corners for women I love

I am not Harvey Specter, but I too pretend to be emotionless sometimes

I am not Dr House, but I know God exists and we keep that faith intact

I am not Don Draper, but I can still sell a refrigerator to you when you don't need it

I am not Joker, but I wish to be the devil many times.

I am not Tony Stark, but I wish I were that wealthy and prosperous

I am not Flash, but I want to be at plenty of places altogether

I am not Wolverine, but I crave to kill people with my claws

I am not Eminem, but I rap good, really good

I am not hot as David Guetta, but I am cool from inside

I am not cool as Ashton Kutcher, but I don't feel hot for it

I don't ride an Aston Martin, but I try hard to reach for it

I am not Alan Walker, but I do imitate his style of hiding face

I am not a fictional character, but I am a funny character.

When women reject me comparing themselves with the fictional characters they adore,

I can admit that I am not him but me.

I can't play many roles.

They are good at being one character whereas I play multiple characters at a time.

They don't notice me for some reason because they have many reasons to be noticed.

I am not a fictional character, but I am a funny character.

Kevin has built a relationship with his stage

"Are you prepared?" asked Zubin.

"Yes, I am all set. I am actually pumped up with all the energy. You know I have been

waiting for this moment."

Results are announced

"As one of the finalists, Kevin is performing again for you…"

Alas! Hope was not to be. It was the twenty-second day of my wife, my guiding star, being in a coma. I was sitting beside her holding her hand. Suddenly, I heard irregular beeps from the monitor.

I ran to get the doctor. I watched my wife slip away from the world in front of my eyes. She breathed her last that day. My world had become dark again. I did not know how my daughter and I would survive without the angel in our lives. A year passed on. I had not stopped grieving. Friends and family said my daughter deserved all my attention, and I should start living life for her sake. It did not make sense to me! I had lost the love of my life. I will never be able to talk to her, hug her, or just hold her hand. I felt empty within.

One day I saw my daughter take her first steps. She walked slowly towards me with a smile on her face. Her eyes had a look of innocence and trust. I cannot break that trust. I realized that my wife had given me the best gift ever, our daughter. I had to look over the horizon and start over. The pain inside me slowly started healing. I still feel incomplete without her, and I know I always will, but I learned to cope with that emptiness and sadness.

When my daughter turned fifteen, I started an organization to help people cope with the loss of loved ones. I know how tough it is and wanted to make sure people had a shoulder to lean on. I think my wife would have liked the idea too. Our daughter, Sakshi, has grown into a wonderful woman today. She is about to join college. So many years have passed since that fateful day. Sakshi has turned out just like her mother. She is mature, fun-loving, and beautiful, and I am proud of her. I know my wife is proud of her too. I hope I meet her if there is an afterlife.

So, friends, it is not what happens in life or how big a tragedy might seem; it is about how you deal with it. Sometimes it may seem that life has been unfair to you, but the truth to a peaceful existence is acceptance. Keep following to know more from the one kissed by the light of wisdom.

Celebrating 10 years of sweet rejections

August 29, 2008 — It all started on this day, the falling apart,

Sneha, her name was, my school crush. Hormones were playing their part.

My first adrenaline rush. Those days, Maturity and Puberty were no art,

Without thinking too much, to her I gave my innocent and decent pumping heart.

While falling for her and fulfilling my desire, I wasn't aware that I was emptying my own cart,

That day, she, without any hesitation, full of cruelty, ripped my soul apart.

Those days, I imagined I could find someone who would call me Sweetheart,

Unfortunately, I had to rest myself in peace and reboot my brain for a restart.

Time passed fast. Intelligence increased very fast, but my face made a U-turn,

If I had to troll me, I would say I looked like some burnt ugly bun,

So, usually and casually, I consoled myself saying, 'I have a sunburn.'

In college, I entered. I made good stylish friends, and thought I would learn,

In the hustle to impress a girl, single girl once in a lifetime, I started to overturn.

No female found me attractive. No one ever fell for me. It was a disastrous feeling,

I understood that I had to get over it and started doing more faith healing.

No sooner did I find it was impossible to do than I started doing something appealing,

I started to write creative, crazy, and weird stuff even though I was doing engineering.

Some clapped smiling — Some clapped laughing — Some clapped looking at the ceiling,

College ended. It was time for earning, settling, and still, I was finding a girl to propose to kneeling.

I wrote and I wrote more, I blogged, I wrote more, I published books, I wrote more,

My magnificent mind fucked emotional heart as there was no girl soul in my store.

I cried. I sobbed. I bawled. I stood dumbstruck. I tried lying on the floor,

It was not too late when I started thinking negatively: 'Every girl is a whore.'

I kept trying. I didn't want to be that loser but the lions always roar,

Tinder. Instagram Chat. Messenger. I failed, and I asked 'What for?'

Plenty of girls talked, smiled, and laughed at my jokes, went far,

In these years, struggling years, I am sure I have raised my bar.

I felt sad about the sudden reality that I could never be anyone's star,

Like my colour skin, I felt I was useless, helpless coal tar.

I am sorry, I say to myself when I hear no patting sound on my shoulder.

In ruthless life, I have heard more I am sorry(s) than Thank you(s) and Love you(s).

Today, on August 29 2018

So, tired of listening to their sorry(s), before they say 'I am sorry, Kevin. You could do more.'

Today I say to myself, 'I am sorry, Kevin, you could not do it. Anymore.'

Uncountable Rejections may not make me strong but celebrating it might.

I proudly say, 'I am an Unproposed Guy.'

Winner Announced

"Kevin, it is."

Kevin just loves the stage

I was washing my clothes, forgot to separate the whites, thought how do I handle all this alone, and started having a quarter-life crisis again. You know, the usual. When suddenly my notification went 'Heyy' in a sweet girl's voice indicating a text message. Yes, that's my text notification, but in my defence, this is my only chance of a girl addressing me personally without asking 'do you I know you?' and then blocking me.

So, I opened it, and alas! There was yet another advertising message telling me to call this number if I want to lose 10 kgs in 10 days. 10 kgs in 10 days! I know most of you would think how stupid this is but let me remind you that India has always been a country of great inventions.

How to be a doctor in 20 days? How to get rid of that monster the society usually calls your husband's mistress? How to top board exams in 5 days (okay, this might be easy if you have political connections). Name it, and it's there. So anyway, being immune to body shaming, such messages do not move me (pun intended). But one part of the message concerned me. "Tired of being single? Lose 10 kgs in 10 days" the whole message read. And immediately, I felt personally attacked for being single.

Anything related to being single, even a small mention, triggers me and sends my mind into a deep analysis mode to discover the greater truth and answer the most important question of my existence: 'Why am I single?' At times like this, I feel sad and desperate (less than the usual). Therefore, I decided to do what every man would want when he feels sad and rejected. No, not that. The second one. I decided to message my ex.

I unlocked my phone and searched for her name, Nisha. "Hey there", my message read. I looked at her display picture and it once again confirmed the law that girls get more beautiful after a breakup or maybe you just seem to value them more after you have lost them but let's just go with the former. She sent back "Oh, hi" after 10 minutes.

"How are you?"

"I am doing good. Wbu?"

"Me too. So, still in Canada?"

"No, actually, I am in India for a wedding." Her text said.

"Oh, that's great. How long would you be here?"

"For another 30–40 days probably."

"Any chance you can give me 2 hours from those 30–40 days?"

"Haha, I guess I can."

"So, free this weekend?"

"Only if you promise to visit that restaurant in Old Delhi."

"Done then."

And the date was set. I was 90% sure it was a dream and I would wake up to my phone singing "Hey honey it's time to get up" which is my alarm tone. Again, don't judge me.

"Do you mind if I bring someone along? You can too. I thought it would be less awkward considering our history." Her message read.

My dream date was gone. I thought of a friend I could take along but immediately remembered the time Ansh and I were on a double date and he said: "Did it hurt when you fell from heaven?" The girl had looked at us in disgust. We never got another date. Therefore, trusting the statistics which say I have never ruined a date, having been on just two, I decided to go alone. And you know what they say, charm her friend and you might impress her easily.

I decided to lightly flirt with her friend so that she likes me and it gets easier for Nisha to like me again. With elaborate planning and self-help books, I was prepared. The day finally came. I dressed in a black shirt and blue jeans and put on Nisha's favourite cologne. I drove to the restaurant and to my surprise, she and her friend were already there. Her friend looked so beautiful that for a second, I decided to change my plan, but my conscience screamed to stick to the current one. Nisha introduced me to her friend called 'J', and all three of us shook hands.

"So, J, do you live in Delhi?"

"No, I am here for Nisha's cousin's wedding. I have heard that if you don't attend their wedding, they won't attend yours." And she winked. Nisha laughed.

"Oh, you are getting married too?"

"Did Nisha not tell you? Nisha and I are getting married in October."

She slid the wedding card towards me, but for a moment, I had gone blind.

"Oh, Congratulations! I am happy for you."

"Would you come to the wedding? Please do. We'll be glad to have you."

"Actually no, I am joining a weight loss program in October. Lose 10 kgs in 10 days."

Kevin, Kevin, Kevin

The show was not boring, but I hadn't heard any song the performer was playing. Also, there were no hot chicks beside, near or around me. The friend who came with me must be devastated as he is handsome enough to score but no such luck! It was already a couple of hours. I wasn't enjoying the songs the performer sang. I went there as I got the tickets for free but as there were no hot girls around me, it was time to leave. I felt it was the most ridiculously wasted time of my life otherwise, as you know, I would have made an impact.

Anyway, we were walking towards the exit when a favourite song of mine began playing. My friend and I chose to go to the other side and stand where we could shake our booty.

Guys were in a group, with girls, and vice versa. It's just a matter of time when we would go out of the park rueful about the lack of beautiful chicks in our lives, especially mine, only mine.

My dude friend was trying to dance towards a group who were as we desis call it 'Bindaas' full of swagger and sensuous moves. On the other hand, I have always known my true 'Aukaat', I was merely moving my hands on the other side. It was just a matter of a few minutes when I recalled the Osho lesson, having visited the Pune Ashram once. The lesson was simple: 'Dance like no one is watching.'

Which brings us to The Beginning of the Failed Dance.

I danced. I danced like no one was watching. I haven't had drugs or weed or alcohol in my life, but I am sure that's how it must feel like. I was so into the dancing, I thought I achieved salvation. I remembered how my dancer friend 'Samrat DC' once expressed his passion and how it has helped him in his personal life.

I had my eyes closed, headbanging, with my spectacles in my hand. I was conscious of my radius. I would bang my legs and stretch my arms. The gym came into effect; the stamina had increased.

That was when my dude friend told me, "Bro, the group beside us is trying to imitate your moves, every move. I am jealous."

It was already 25 minutes that I was headbanging. I didn't turn back to see who was following my steps. I started with my dance again, considering the fact that I should remain in salvation, ignoring the human psyche.

After a few minutes, as expected, three guys from the group, approached me, asking, "What's your name? Where are you from?" The answer was very calm, gentle, and polite. I still remember the looks and respect those young guys of the second semester of engineering gave me. I also remember the No look and No Respect from the girls. I felt oblivious, obviously.

It was my saturation. The stamina lowered. The energy, the momentum fell. Gravity succeeded. I sat down on the ground.

I looked at myself, perspiration pelted me, felt like the fountains of heaven. I looked around, girls beautiful as angels, felt out of the league for me. I smiled to myself. I went to all the boys to say goodbye. I stopped myself. I didn't go to any of the girls. I turned back, telling my friend, "The white top chick was looking at you. Go approach her."

I walked alone, in the midst of the crowd, not a single person looking at me, not a single individual praising the madness I showed in dancing, not a pat, not a word of praise. I turned back. Like the tiger in Life of Pi doesn't care about his master when he reaches his jungle, I felt I would never be respected or applauded being a common man, no matter how hard I would work or how miraculous my work would seem. It's all about 'an unknown force' that drives you to do the impossible.

We left. My friend was busy discussing the 'failed attempt' with the girl he approached. I was dumbstruck in 'The Failed Dance' I did.

5

The Blast from the Past

"Kevin, are you done here? Let's watch the show."

"Show, Ansh?" Kevin turned away from the unknown people and looked at him inquisitively.

"Yes, Zubin has planned something. Come on, let's go!"

Zubin's name made his stomach flip. He had been on edge barely keeping himself calm but now he wondered what extravaganza his brother might have picked to show off at his wedding. Not having any choice, however, he took a seat with his friends for the live show.

"And here comes the groom! Welcome! How are you? I am Pulkit J, your entertainer for this evening. No, I am not a dancer, not a singer. I am a stand-up comedian." He smiled widely. "Yes, a stand-up comedian at a wedding! Sounds wonderful, doesn't it? So, please sit back and let's have some fun!"

The performer waited for the applause to die down. "When you go to a typical Indian wedding, what do you see? Lots of colours, decoration, people laughing, dancing, but well that's on the outside. If you get closer and look deeper, you will see girls bitching about what the bride is wearing or the other cousin's make-up is too bold, the middle-aged aunties will be the ones slaying the dance floor, you know, with their panting breaths and falling sarees.

"Then there are the young boys, checking out the young girls, deciding among themselves, the one in red is mine, the one in green you take. As if the girls are candies and the boys are merely distributing it among themselves. You take this colour, my favourite is this one, so I take this. They will divide between all; no man is left behind. As if the moment they will say, "Oh, I like this red colour you are wearing," she will go with him, no questions asked. He likes that colour no, what more is there to know?

"And the uncles, you will always find them at the food counter. Due to their health or age, their wives don't allow them spicy food or sweets, so they pack up on those when at a wedding. As it is, the wife is busy on the dance floor. They attack a gulab jamun like they are stuck on this island alone and this piece is the last remaining food item. What will they eat after this? Where will they get food from now on… Such a dilemma.

"The bride or groom is the most lost soul. They are nervous about the day or need a break from the noise or some peace, but that's not possible as people keep coming—this cousin, that Aunty, that Aunty's Aunty—they have to keep smiling and laughing for all the guests and the photos. It is so scary at times—what if their teeth fall out?

"And we all know how kids today are so obsessed with selfies. I want to meet the guy who invented this trend. I mean, when they wake up, they want to click selfies and post it, saying 'morning look'. At least brush your teeth, one can smell your morning breath from the selfie. But no, taking a selfie and posting has become more important now.

"While they workout they want to post a selfie, while they eat, with their dogs, with lovers or even while doing nothing, like sitting under the sun. I fear sometimes a day will soon come when I shall see someone posting a selfie while sitting on the toilet or even while making love in the bedroom. No privacy, no limits. I even heard cases wherein people have gone to Marine Drive so desperate to take a good selfie with the rising tide that they keep going towards the wave and some have even fallen in and died, but people won't stop trying. No matter what, the world goes upside down, whether one lives or dies, that perfect selfie with the tide must happen. It is so appalling!"

"Kevin, you listening to me?" Tina tapped on his shoulder as he roused himself out of his thoughts, his mind having tuned out the performer.

"Huh?" Kevin blinked and focused on his sister.

"Do you want a cola?" She repeated, wondering if her brother was really okay. He seemed lost.

Since his sister was the only family he was close to, he could tell she looked concerned. He could talk to her if he wished, but he simply shook his head. "Uh, no thanks, Tina."

"Kids, are you having fun?" Kevin looked at his mother who seemed attentive of his friends today; it came as quite a surprise to him.

"My Zubin has organised it all." And just as quickly, his hopes came crashing down. Of course it was about Zubin, everything is always about him. Kevin knew his mother had a soft corner for his brother, she never hid it, always boosting her elder son's greatness to people. Her successful and brilliant son who was not Kevin.

"Yes, Aunty." A couple of his friends replied.

"Weddings are so much simpler now." Kevin's mother said, smiling at them. "I recall even till a few years back, they used to be so extravagant. Now, it is only three or four days; earlier, the ceremonies would start ten, even fifteen days before the wedding. Everyone used to stay together, prepare for the wedding together, enjoyed the entire wedding festivities; we had so much fun. Do you remember kids, your Sami Aunty's wedding? You were so little then. That was such a lavish celebration."

Kevin remembered the day, it was hot. Some women were playing the dhol, some were dancing. Mummy was busy ironing Zubin's new suit with the stylish bowtie. Papa was at the drinks counter with the other uncles, chatting away and enjoying the party. Sami Aunty was looking adorable. Just a day left for her wedding. She was laughing and relishing her sangeet ceremony. There was food, music, dancing, and the smell of henna all around. Everyone was having a delightful time. Well, except, Kevin.

"Kevin, come here, let's have a jalebi."

"Tina, please stay here. Let's not mess around." Younger Kevin had pleaded.

But Tina would not budge. "No, let's go. You are so annoying. I am only asking for a jalebi!"

"Okay."

"Sami Aunty is looking so pretty. I will also marry my charming prince one day." Tina said.

"Yeah, right."

"You shall see."

6

The First Encounter

Kevin always thought she looked beautiful, but on this day, she looked stunning. Cousin Piya's best friend, Rita. Kevin was delighted to see her at the sangeet ceremony of his aunt. Should he get her a jalebi too? Or maybe something to drink? A cola? The way she spoke, the way she walked, the way she blushed. Her laugh and her melodious voice continued to linger in his ears. Her shiny hair and the glow on her face. Should he talk to her? No, he couldn't. What if she hated him?

Tina too was looking in their direction but for a different reason. "Kevin, let's see what cousin Piya and others are playing there."

"No, you carry on. I am fine here." Kevin was least interested. He preferred being by himself.

"C'mon!" She pulled on his arm and dragged him to her cousins who were playing together.

"Guys, what are you playing, can we join?" she asked eagerly.

"Yes, but you have to keep it a secret." Piya replied immediately.

"Why?"

"We are going to play an unusual game."

"That's interesting."

"Get inside the room," Their cousin instructed.

"No, Tina, we are leaving. If anyone catches us, mummy won't spare us!" A panicked Kevin was already feeling sweaty.

"Kevin, I want to play! I am not leaving!" He had no other choice but to accompany Tina. She was adamant.

"Shush everyone. Sit down in a circle." They did as they were told.

"Now, I will spin this bottle around and we shall see where it lands. The two facing each end of the bottle shall have to kiss."

Kevin panicked. "I am not playing this, Tina!" He couldn't understand how Tina could be so liberal, knowing well that he would never do such a thing.

"Oh, don't be a spoilsport. Let's see how it goes." Tina chided.

"Okay, so all of you ready? Here we go…"

"Oh, that's Rishabh and Seema."

"Guys, kiss, kiss…yeah!" Everyone chanted enthusiastically.

"Okay, next." She spun the bottle again. "It is, Rita and Kevin."

Oh my god, kiss her? was all Kevin could think. She was the most beautiful girl in the room. How could he? Would she feel bad? Why was he so nervous? He could feel his heart pounding. He was sweaty. He wanted to check if his breath stank, if everything was going to be alright, if he could really do this. Deep breaths in and staying calm. He never wanted to forget this moment and shut his eyes for a second to take a mental image.

"No way, I am not kissing him." He heard Rita say and his eyes snapped open.

"That's the rule, Rita."

"No, I will kiss Adi instead."

What? thought Kevin. He felt embarrassed, angry and irritated all at the same time.

"Here. There you go." Adi obliged.

"Okay. That was…uhh, okay. Hard luck, Kevin."

"A bad day, Kevin."

"Such a dismissal."

"I am not playing anymore, Tina, let's leave." Kevin just could not face anyone in the room. He knew he had to leave immediately and never come back.

"But Kevin, my turn never came," his sister whined.

Kevin pulled Tina out before slamming the door behind him. He was agitated and sad.

Outside, he smelt turmeric, strong and overwhelming. Sami Aunty was seated on the new chair. The women were applying turmeric paste on her body one by one and blessing her with a successful marriage and a positive future. She smiled for the photographers. The giggles, pomp and colour, all shone in the daylight.

Kevin stared, thinking it would never happen to him. Maybe, the world did not deserve him. Perhaps he had his hopes up too high. He was better alone, solo. He likened himself to the Hulk, powerful always.

★ ★ ★

"Kevin? I am asking you." Zubin shook Kevin awake from his reverie.

"Huh. What, Zubin?"

"Do you remember Sangeetha, our cousin from Dehradun? She is here to meet you." Zubin looked slightly annoyed but had his features schooled to look like a polite host for others.

"Yes, of course."

"Congratulations, Kevin. How are you feeling? Meet my husband," Sangeetha said.

"Hi, hey guys." He replied with an awkward wave.

"Don't mind but you missed our wedding. It was perfect. We finally got married after five years in a relationship; we were college sweethearts. I still recall the day in college when he told me he had a crush on me. Oh, he was so nervous, so cute. Ah, I was already in love with him. I couldn't have said no."

"Sangeetha, let's get something to eat." Her husband interrupted. Kevin just smiled at Sangeetha, thinking he was as lucky as her now. He was marrying his chosen sweetheart and felt truly blessed.

"Okay, yes. Fine, Kevin, have a great day!"

7

The First Crush

Kevin was thinking of his high school crush, how amazing she looked that day. He had promised himself no more girls, he had vowed to be solo, but what could he do? As she walked, the place lit up, it seemed, even in the daytime. It was rose day at school. Every guy had chosen the girl to whom they wanted to give a rose. Kevin too considered his options. Would she take it, would she throw it, or would she laugh at him? But when he spotted her, he knew he was ready to give her the rose, to confess his feelings to her. As he started walking towards her, the world around him blurred. He could see only her and no one or nothing else. She turned towards him and before he could say anything, he heard her say, "Keep this with the others on my table, will you?"

Only then he noticed she had a table full of roses. Then why would she like his any better? She didn't even look back, she didn't even smile, she didn't even say thank you. He felt his heart shatter. Why? Why him?

"Kevin, there's your Kumar Uncle, look at him dance between your sister and her friends. Such youthfulness in old age." Said Ansh.

Kevin blinked back to the present.

"Yeah, let his wife leave the food counter and see him, then we will see his youthfulness!" Dev chuckled.

"Guys, come on, let's dance. Kevin, you too." Kabir said, waiting for his friends to join him.

"You know I can't dance!" Kevin felt goosebumps run across his body.

"Chill, it's your wedding day, you have to dance." All his friends said with determination.

Feeling too self-conscious, he shook his head. "Guys, no, please."

"Yes, Kevin, we will make you dance today. Shake that booty. Yeah."

They ended up making him dance. Finally.

8

Trust Me, I Can't Dance!

"Bro, thanks for doing this on my birthday. I realize it has been challenging for you. But you know my girl too, she wanted this." Dev said, looking apologetic and grateful at the same time.

"Yes, it is killing me." Kevin gave a nod and said. "You are very well aware how awful I am at this."

"Just one day more, Kevin. Tomorrow it shall all be over. Your practise will pay off." Kevin knew his friends meant a lot to him and hence he was doing this to only to help a friend else he would never dream of doing something like this his entire life.

It was all a blur. The stage seemed set, a bright light was blinding him and he could hear the cheers of the crowd. They stood in their positions, waiting. Kevin closed his eyes for a few seconds, and suddenly the music started. Breathing hard, he tried to move ahead, tried to remember the steps, and looked at others to calm his nervousness. He was dancing on the stage, a birthday gift to Dev. His friends, their girlfriends, Tina and Kevin, a group dance on a pub stage. This should be recorded as the most unique gift ever given to a friend. Kevin had rehearsed with Tina, but dancing was not his forte and it would never be. As he struggled on the stage, he could see everyone else perform amazingly well.

He was pretty confident that things might go downhill due to him, that his incredibly poor performance would ruin the whole act. He did the only thing he could think of to avoid being seen dancing shoddily: he kept himself hidden behind the rest as much as he could. But his luck soon ran out and he slipped on the next step of having to turn away from his partner, his elbow hitting her nose severely. Tina yelled as she had started bleeding from the broken nose. Everything was a blur again. Kevin swore he would never try to dance on the stage again.

He shivered, recollecting the past.

"Now it is time for your initial groom rituals. Some ceremony for you and your ghodi…" Kevin's mother informed suddenly appearing in front of him.

"What?" He asked anxiously, not enjoying his present and constantly seeking solace in an uncomfortable past.

"Yes, c'mon."

"Okay, now Kevin, stand straight next to it. I will run this aarti in front of you two."

"Mummy, what is this? Is this necessary?" Kevin knew for his parents the age old, not making any sense rituals mattered more than anything else.

"I wouldn't do it if it wasn't. Now, would I?" she said sounding annoyed.

"Uh." Kevin did not believe in these weird customs but he could not say no to his mother whom he loved despite her preference for her other son. So he stood next to the ghodi and allowed his mother to do as she pleased while he let his thoughts take over.

9

Why Me?

"Kevin, we have to go." Ansh said.

"Yes, we all are going; we will not leave you behind." Dev nodded, urging him.

Kevin's friends had a night out planned but he did not want to be a part of it due to his past experiences of embarrassment and awkwardness.

"No, Dev, you guys carry on. I am not going."

"Come on, there will be lights, drinks, fun, and girls."

"Pretty girls. We have planned to meet up with some girls from college when we get there."

"Yes, Kevin. Please don't spoil our plan."

"We have already talked our parents into letting us go too." One of his friends urged.

"Okay." He reluctantly agreed as he didn't want to let them down. Their words of encouragement had also helped. After all, why shouldn't he spend the night out with his friends, enjoying himself?

"Let's get ready guys and meet outside my house." Kabir suggested and they dispersed.

Kevin got dressed. He felt strangely positive. Maybe today was the day of no rejection; maybe today ought to be a good day, maybe today was the day he would meet a girl meant for him.

The entrance was lit with neon lights. Boldly shining on the top were the words Blue Light Disco. So many people just moving around, some lost in each other, some forgotten in their own bodies, and some washing away their life struggles with dancing. Kevin and his friends had made a pact: a little alcohol, a little dancing with the girls, and then back home. If anyone got lucky, that is a different case. Within minutes his friends were dancing with their partners, some girls who were just chilling, and he was left alone on the side, drinking his little martini. Gazing across the dance floor, it felt the same: the same world, the same loneliness, the same him.

Then, he noticed a hand in front of him. He rubbed his eyes and it was still there. A girl was asking him to dance with her. She looked sane, not drugged in any way. Did she really want to?

You want to dance? she asked.

Kevin could only nod, continuously staring at her, nervous about her nearness.

In no time they were dancing together. She moved closer and put her arms around him and his panic grew. It felt chilly, vibrant, noisy, calm, all at the same time. Kevin had her all to himself. Was she real?

Suddenly he heard loud chuckling, clapping and hooting. Kevin opened his eyes and realised he was dancing alone. The others looked at him, laughing while his friends tried to hide their faces. His eyes were still searching for her when he heard the chants of *I won, I won!* The one he had been looking for was shouting in glee. It was now all clear to him; it was a dare to dance with him. He was nothing but a bet. Should he rebel, should he revolt, should he feel sorry for himself or should he gloat? It was all a blur.

"Kevin?"

He jumped slightly. "Uh, yes, Papa?"

"The travel agency guys have sent in your trip confirmation. I will share them with you later." He looked at his son curiously then looked away, never giving his second son any attention more than what was needed. Kevin's father was a simple man with idealistic values. For him it was always about taking care of the family.

"Sure, Papa."

"There are the e-ticket, the e-visa, and other trip itinerary details."

"Okay."

"Son?"

"Huh. Yes, yes, Papa." Kevin brought his wandering mind to a halt once again.

"I was saying your passport is with me. Don't forget that."

"Fine."

He knew his father would take care of all the essential tasks at the wedding. He knew he feared a bad reputation and it could also be something he wanted to do for his son for a change. Kevin hoped.

10

Life and Death

"Kevin, we are leaving, quick! Tony Uncle has passed away. Major heart stroke. We are going to his funeral now." Tina hollered.

"What? B-but he has two young daughters. And his old mother too. How will Ria Aunty take care of it all? Oh, he was so young. That's so sad."

"Kevin, are you crying?"

"No, Tina, I am not. I am just feeling bad for Tony Uncle and his family." Kevin was an emotional person. There was nothing wrong with it. He could understand the importance of life and death together at such times.

"Don't you ever feel why so much of life if it has to go in an instant someday? What is the point of it all? The relationships or the sacrifices, as one day all of it will be forgotten. The reality is in the end what one has, what one loves or holds dear will one day no longer exist. It is common sense. Everybody knows someday they will die. So, it is eminent that you feel it and accept it."

"Ugh, Kevin, whatever." Tina rolled her eyes. "I don't want to be so negative. I am worried about my annual school drama, which is tomorrow. I want to stay happy and optimistic."

"You will never understand, Tina." For Tina, nothing was ever a big deal; she never fussed over anything. Kevin often wondered if he was the only one who cared in this family.

"Kevin, mummy and papa are here. Let's go; the photographer needs some wide family shots. We are all needed there."

He got up and followed his sister who appeared to care, for a change.

"Yeah, okay." Kevin seemed ready to take some family pictures on his D-day.

11

Three Is a Crowd

"Kevin, faster, please. They must be waiting for us."

"Ansh, I have come only for you. You know that."

"Yes, and thank you. I owe you a big one bro. But I told you, my girl wouldn't come alone, and she didn't want her friend to be alone while we enjoyed the movie. You know what I mean. So, here you are to give the friend some company."

While the wedding shenanigans continued, Kevin recollected the day he and Ansh were on their way to a movie date and running a little behind. Kevin was a little uncomfortable but also looking forward to it. The things you do for your friends, but you also never know where you might meet that someone special.

"Hey, Bani. Here, meet my good friend, Kevin."

Bani beamed at them. "Hi Kevin, this is Srishti."

"Great." Kevin mumbled and tried a smile.

"Let me get some popcorn and cola. There is still time for the movie to start." Ansh said and he and Bani left.

"So, Kevin, what do you major in?" Srishti gave him a small, polite smile.

"Civil engineering."

"Okay." They looked around them quietly.

"What do you do? I mean, what are you studying?" Kevin asked to fill the awkward silence.

"I am majoring in fashion designing."

"Nice." He felt nervous, feeling empty of topics already. "The movie should be good, I heard. It's about the protagonist's best friend dying of terminal illness while they both try and do whatever he had wished to do before he dies."

"Hmm." Srishti pursed her lips, pretending to pay attention but wished she were somewhere else.

"You know how it is, life and death, it is all a cycle that teaches us, inspires us to make the most of it through adventures and friendship as you shall lose yourself in their journey at some point. It is like being in the will of nothingness. So, you need to embrace the void, feel moved, and then show that cold, unfeeling world what you are aiming for, in life." Kevin droned on, the silence from his date making it even more awkward.

"Huh."

When Ansh and Bani came back Srishti looked visibly relieved. "Listen, Bani. I am not spoiling your date. But who has your friend come with? Such a weirdo. I cannot sit next to him. Please. I will sit next to you only. I promise I will not disturb you. Please."

"Okay, fine."

As they settled in for the movie, Kevin realised maybe this was a day of no rejection, maybe it was to be a good day, maybe it was the day he met a girl meant for him. Only, she walked away and sat next to a stranger instead of next to him. But it didn't bother him anymore. He had a feeling this might happen. He knew he was ready for yet another rejection. Suddenly, so much of his quirky, odd, misunderstood behaviour had meaning. There was nothing wrong with him. He was simply an introvert. Being around people drained his batteries. He craved some me-time to do some reflecting, some processing and just to give himself some momentum. He was shy with girls but did not lack self-esteem. He was not even anti-social. He desired to learn new things, take new risks, explore and develop his life. He merely needed some solitude to recharge. And if he did not get sufficient doses of this me-time, his spirit would suffer, turning him into what the girls called 'the weirdo geek'.

With her sharp tongue, his mother succeeded in bringing him back to the present.

"Kevin, at least today you could have got rid of these rings on your face!"

"Oh, Mummy." He shut his eyes in rejection, willing himself to be patient.

"It's just horrifying. It is your wedding today! You could have cleaned up better today."

"But Mummy…"

Speaking over him, she said, "Look at my Zubin, so cultured and civilized; he looks so handsome." Kevin felt a chill run down his spine. It was always about Zubin for his mother. He knew it but could not react to it. He had to hold his fist tight to drown some of the growing aggression.

"He is not looking like a hippie, you know, like you." She added after a pause.

He looked away from her, grinding his jaw shut.

Kevin's Feats

The stage is his best friend – Part I

Relationships are messy. Oh, you might already know that. I also know this, no not from my own experience but because of my observational power that is one of the best traits of my personality, apart from being funny, of course.

My failure in the area of relationships has helped me in a certain way, like Thomas Alva Edison had said, "I have not failed. I have just found 10,000 ways that won't work." Thanks to my failure, I have a list of things not to do in a relationship.

1.Lie.

Most of you would say this is cliché. But still, we, as a tribe, continue to do that. You might think your lies are justified, but you shouldn't overestimate your sense of judgment. For e.g., lying because you have a birthday surprise for her is justified but lying to her that you did not smoke so you don't fight isn't a rightful one no matter how much you think otherwise.

2. Make your girlfriends jealous.

Only boys make their girlfriends jealous and not men. While you think her getting jealous shows how much she loves/likes you, it can also show how she is feeling a lack of love. Learning from over-smart men who lost their relationships just because they took their girlfriend's insecurity as a joke, I strictly recommend not to do so.

3.Not choosing your media.

The media has been constantly feeding us an idea of a perfect relationship and a perfect bachelor life. Do not believe it. If your idea of love life is inspired by Pyaar ka Punchnama, then let me burst your bubble, you don't get a fancy rant of a monologue in real life. From Kajol choosing SRK over Salman in Kuch Kuch Hota Hai even though he had friend-zoned her and chosen the other, more beautiful chick, to Jimmy Shergil in basically every movie, media's idea of love is pretty skewed. No, singing in a public place would not get you a girl, and maybe you should start with this lesson while choosing what influences your mind and ultimately your love language.

4.Ownership.

No matter how fancy the 'I own' and 'Aww, all yours' tags sound on Instagram, the real world does not appreciate ownership. When you are in a relationship, try to think of you and your girlfriend as partners and not you owning her or vice versa. Give each other the space you require and help them grow as a person. If being in a relationship, you aren't a better version of yourself or you feel that you are constantly under pressure to behave in a certain way, then maybe it's time to embrace singlehood again.

5. Not recognizing the red flags early.

"When you look at someone with rose-coloured glasses, all the red flags look just like…flags," Wanda from Bojack horseman once said.

You need to remember your relationship isn't your diet. You don't need to defend it every time. Trust is an important part of a relationship, but it shouldn't be doled out blindly. You need to recognise the red flags early in the relationship or those might be the reasons for the end. For example, if your partner always seems busy and does not put in efforts to talk to you or if she thinks that yelling at you and getting her way around is 'cute' then you might want to reconsider your relationship.

That's all for now. Will keep on adding to this list as I am pretty sure my love life isn't going to witness a miracle anytime soon.

The stage is his best friend – Part II

Ever since Badshah's 'Mercy' song came out, almost every guy became a regular at the club in hopes of finding that "sabse alag" girl. So, it would be a no-brainer to guess where one can find me in the evenings. Well, let's face it, only cool rappers like Badshah can tell us where to find our dream girl; please don't confuse it with Hema Malini, because that would be wrong on so many levels.

Anyway, unlike Badshah and probably every other guy on this planet, the problem with me is my stars are permanently doomed. And not just for one particular reason. First of all, for better or worse, I found one sabse alag girl every evening. Every evening I had a different idea of my dream girl. However, to my utter dismay, every one of those girls not only found me ordinary, but also a creep. I mean, I know my way of showing interest is weird, but Badshah didn't exactly hand us any manual for this.

Nevertheless, one such evening, I thought I had ultimately found my sabse alag girl and just for a little while, assumed my stars were finally shining. Little did I know my doomed stars had decided to humiliate me further that evening!

There I was sitting with my friends at the bar, waiting for our next round of drinks, when a friend of mine pointed me to our 10 o'clock where a group of girls were looking in our direction and laughing. It's not that I hadn't noticed them earlier, but I knew those girls were way beyond our league. Especially mine, who couldn't form a single proper sentence while talking to a girl, let alone trying to impress her.

But that night, I gathered courage, or rather vodka courage, and along with my friends approached the girls. I was more confident about the fact that since I was with friends, I would not have to do much talking. Nodding, smiling, and occasionally saying yes or no would work. Almost all of us had selected one girl for ourselves to impress.

And, like I said another score for my doomed stars, the girl that was with me turned out to be the silent-listening types. While she tried to start several conversations, I was unable to form more than one-line answers to her questions. Peeking around, I saw that almost everyone except us was having fun.

Just then, the song of the hour was played, and it was Mercy. Finally, I said to hell with it and turned around to ask the girl if she would like to dance, only to see her walking to the dance floor with some random guy. If that humiliation was not enough, I saw that all our friends were joking and laughing at me.

After that, I quietly went back to the bar and drank for the next hour alone. After what felt like an eternity my friends returned, clapping each other's shoulders and boasting how they got their girl's number or a day and time for a second date. As if the quota of my humiliation that night was not enough, they all started consoling me and telling me how they would help me score next time.

That day I decided there was no real Mercy for an unfortunate soul like me.

Stage is the only friend in difficult times, for Kevin

On an irregular odd day, the Head and the Heart had a great fight,

Had I not taken it seriously, it could have been a little light.

The Head was hammering,

The Heart was stammering.

The Head had brain,

But the Heart was fully trained.

Head said I would stop working if you fall for someone, 'good' for you,

Heart said never mind; nobody's gonna fall, I am not silly.

That day,

The Head was stunned and furious.

Said, "Heart, you betrayed me. We're together. Don't leave me. How could you do this?"

Heart said, "I didn't do anything. But yesterday, one heart from another universe helped me pump more, gave me more blood, had me more adrenaline, and made me feel like I am special. And now, I feel I will stop pumping, if you scare me, d***head."

That day, the Heart won, as always, and two hearts went into a different universe as always.

The stage always saves Kevin from having a complete bad day

Let me tell you about this one time, when I was alone with a girl in an elevator and it suddenly stopped. The security alarm had already been raised. It was a matter of time we had to go through. She succeeded, I failed.

No, No. I am not going to be erotic. Definitely not with how the 50 shades of grey showed the audience what can possibly happen in an elevator. It's just a different unromantic story. As I said, you know the end, I don't make it somehow, but except that, you need to know how it is to be with (I don't know about 'On' or 'Below') a girl, observing silently and sometimes, talking, I'm sorry, rather, murmuring to yourself.

*The first few minutes were just the unconscious state of mind where we feared death but then we realized it's not a horror movie. The next minute we took out our smartphones, to call the concerned person. Seriously? I still dialled the f***ing 10 digits to call my friends and families. I didn't have any useful numbers. I was a douche. I am not saying it, she must have said that when she asked me if I had any relevant, helpful number.*

By the time I nodded, I felt so optimistic about the situation as if I had a few saved numbers. I think we even got married in my imagination. Yes, certainly, she wasn't impressed with my looks, because duh, you are bald at the age of 25, and who wears toilet slippers outside the house?

God hears of those who help others, right?

I finally got my moment, I call it, the "Masturbation Moment" where some scene would occur to me and I would save it for its later use. I had to lift her up since we were on midway floors. Catching her from the waist, thin waist, softly thin waist, I lift her on the lift and don't guess what lifted itself eventually?

Not a single word was spoken. I felt dumbstruck, disgusted and dead. I managed to get out of that cubicle hell that made me look a fool to a beautiful girl.

Stage is where Kevin can be his own self

> "We have heard that Kevin is an aficionado of Game of Thrones. Guys and girls, can we hear some cheer for GOT rap!"
>
> "Kevin, Kevin, Kevin, Kevin…!"
>
> "The Unproposed Guy is a big fan of Game of Thrones. Well, recite it, recite it…"
>
> Enter into the world of chaos, the jungle of bizarre
>
> Where combat is a religion, and ceasefire is cowardliness
>
> Where killing is sacred, and birth is profane
>
> Where layman are slaves, and a dwarf is a leader
>
> Where vengeance is mandatory, and forgiveness is rare
>
> Where slaughtering is holy, and freedom is just temporary
>
> Where reals falls like cards, and cardholders are deceived
>
> Where ghosts are real, and fairy tales are a myth
>
> Where fear is death; but dead do awake
>
> Where the sun shines no brighter, and the moon is long-lasting
>
> Where the old stories don't repeat, and the new ones don't cast
>
> Where magic ain't an illusion, and skin-changing is existing

Where angels don't visit often; but witches sojourn frequently

Where fortune-telling is authentic, and satanism is undeniable

Where emotion isn't a feeling and hunger isn't starving

Where wolves protect, and ravens assist

Where traitors are subtle; but loyalists ignorant

Where eunuchs guide people, and the shrewd manipulate

Where family feud is apparent, and illegitimacy is patronized

Where sex is just lust, and rape ain't a crime

Where kindness kills; but wickedness saves

Where selfishness is for safety and greed is not cupidity

Where one minute it's love, and the other minute its hate

Where butchery and massacre are tamed, and fortitude is handicapped

Where money is not prosperity; but bloodshed is the measure of maturity

Where addiction is not considered a bad habit, and dependency is the worst

Where fire can't burn a dragon, but ice slays snowmen

Whose side are you on?

*Shut up! Cause they don't give a F****

The stage and Kevin are now inseparable

I didn't know I would do it to this extent. I certainly couldn't believe what I saw. I had no idea what to do with it, and so, I'm sharing it with you guys and girls of Tinder age. It was that midnight when I completed a year but was unable to celebrate the anniversary, it was a 365-day completion of my Tinder installation, and I had not been able to find a single date.

Adding salt to my misery, the roommate told me, "Bhai, you owe me 300 something bucks. You subscribed for some shit and all."

Yes, I had told my friend that it was a Hotstar subscription and he would always wonder why I would deny sharing my smartphone for an hour or so to watch the GOT episodes. It turned out that day he found out that I had purchased the paid version of Tinder and he freaked out.

*"Saala, dost to chu**ya banata hai. How many dates did you find in this one month?"*

Soon after he realized I couldn't find any date from the paid version, there was a 2-minutes silence in our apartment, and we decided to make use of that one last day of the paid application.

This is how we did it: The unexpected search of all the 'Un-dated Guys' like me whom I gave the name 'The Unproposed Guys'.

Since we had the paid version of the app, we turned our settings from finding 'Female' to finding 'Male' and went on to check the entire categories of guy profiles across the country. We changed locations, we changed ages, and we changed settings to get 'That One Guy' who was like us—funniest, weirdest and ugliest, and boy were we in for a surprise!

There were no such profiles, there were many. Guys become salesmen when they show off. I will start with one of the primary profiles which excited us both to make that night the most memorable and laughable.

1) 'Swipe Right To Know More, Dear.'

Wow, this is the worst and the slowest clickbait ever. The guy is so confident the girl will swipe him right though he had three pictures of 'Shree Ganesh', 'Shree Krishna' and 'Vishnu' in his profile. May the lords bless him and his bait!

2) 'Hit me up if you feel so, baby.'

That's what I wanted to do. The TED talk taught me to have confidence, but even I didn't get the guts to say this in a virtual world where only women will read it, only women. After this, I came across many irrelevant phrases that made no sense but were written so dauntlessly that I 'laughed on my feet', yea, this kind of phrase.

3) 'I am here for a few days only, ladies. Hurry up.'

"Where is the loudspeaker we haven't used since ages, Samrat?" He turned it on, and I laughed it out with the mic in my hand until he turned it off because I felt relieved and relaxed. Yes, I am not the only stupidest guy in the world. Actually, the world is full of them. Hurry up? Seriously? Didn't I tell you about the sales pitch? Hence, proved.

Within 3 hours and let me profess that they were certainly quite memorable, we had travelled to 15 countries and scrolled almost 500 profiles that were utter bullshit. When I told my friend in excitement, "Drinks on me, tomorrow", only then, I realized that we were already high without alcohol. Man, I haven't expressed my honest emotions sober. He said, "I am proud of you." We hugged laughing, for about two seconds, but then we remembered that we saw a few cool profiles too and we hugged again, crying.

Moving on.

*4) 90s lover. Let's meet at your balcony. I will be downstairs. WhatsApp me: 84600342**'*

5) 'I am getting married soon, but I don't want my wife to tell me that I didn't have any girlfriend to date, so let's date.'

6) 'My mother forced me to register on shaadi.com & my father told me to come here.'

7) 'People are talking about this app. Let's try it. Who wants to date me first?'

I told Samrat to bring the mic, but he denied it. I somehow managed to laugh monstrously enough to wake the neighbours up. This apartment is full of bachelors, so whatever.

8) 'Dheeraj. My name is slow, but I am not. Email me @dheeraj. notsoslow@gmail.com'

9) 'Jignesh. Gujju but I don't like gathiya, fafda or garba. Date me, please, I am cute.'

Man, you should love all those things. Where is your dignity? Be proud of being a Gujju. Before I could buck him up telepathically, Samrat reminded me when I ate egg (being Jain) just to convince a girl (which eventually didn't work out) that I am not afraid of hens.

10) 'Gayrish. I am gay. My gf doesn't know it. Need a girl with whom I can share my feelings because guys don't listen to me anymore.'

Kevin is everything on a stage, a young boy, a teen, a matured person

School days are amazing. It's next to impossible to not have any memories of it, good or bad.

Some would be born Don, some would be born Johny Sins, some would be born Posh, some would always be fighting like Kangana, and there's always a Karan Johar.

Aur ek hota hai Love Guru…

Back then there was no tinder, so they were in huge demand. I am sure this is where the concept of Partner, the movie, came from. Of course when it came to payment, it wasn't with money or weed, you just had to complete their homework. Life was so simple back then!

The stage always accepts Kevin for who he is

There was no room for errors. The stage was set. The play was about to start. The audience was waiting for the most-awaited main event of the school. How could there be any error in this occasion of innocent souls?

It wasn't an annual function. It wasn't a farewell event. It wasn't a fresher's party. It was Children's Day. The title read: Children's Story.

A 5-year-old kid then came to the mic and spoke:

Accept us as we are. Please, don't scare us unnecessarily,

Support us in what we want to do desperately.

Motivate us when we fall immaturely,

Hold us in troubled times. We are sure it's temporary.

My poem may not rhyme every time. But I always try,

I do homework. I long for the cricket bat for my papa to buy.

I become sad, and sometimes I cry,

Let us be us. Let a child be a child.

Dedicated To,

All the children whose confidence can move mountains,

Every little one whose hopes sprinkle like fountains.

The Aspiring Authors, Painters, Guitarist, Engineers & Doctors.

The Unconventional Round Peg in a Square Hole.

Optimism

She giggled as he slipped over a patch of ice on the sidewalk of Snow World. She didn't know her laughter would not last long. Sahil was in pain. Jenny carefully gave him a hand to stand up, but when she heard his groan while getting up, she knew his leg must be fractured.

All the way to the hospital, the nurse watched both of them.

"Jenny in her wheelchair and God forbid…" the nurse stopped her imagination.

The basic treatment was already given in the van. They were about to reach the hospital.

Jenny's face lost its shine and Sahil's shine faded away while looking at her. He screamed without halting, and the nurse couldn't get hold of her negative thoughts; however, she managed.

"Boyfriend-girlfriend?" the nurse asked.

"Yes."

"Since?"

"3 Years."

When they arrived at the hospital, the nurse asked Jenny, "What if he has to face the same situation as yours?"

Jenny said, "It doesn't matter. I met him 3 years ago when he saw me lying on the road. By the way, it was a patch of ice, nurse, not a 100 km/hour car that thrashed him."

The stage is Kevin's bro as well

Unlike others, I don't want to turn back time.

But I wish I could fast forward than rewind,

So I could see me with you at the right time.

And I finally see what I have ever dreamt of.

I might be polite but I'm passionate.

I may fall but don't mind, I have a cushion.

And my shoulder waits for your head to rest.

Like your lap waits for my head to give me the peace.

I turned back again just not to look at her.

This time, to look at her more beautifully.

Here are her mesmerizing eyes looking for me too.

I am going to become hers forever.

If you thought I am in love with you because you are beautiful, you're wrong.

If you thought I missed you when you're not around me, you're wrong.

If you thought my passion for you would decrease with time, you're wrong

and

If you thought you would never think what I think, you're right.

Today, you go into your dreams as you read and hear this.

One day, you will make me fall asleep with your words.

Kevin and the stage are like family

A strong wind but not a cyclone.

A wit inside me sings a song, "She moves her body like a cyclone…"

She was a strong wind but not a hurricane or a cyclone,

Dressed in a long loose dress made of nylon.

Not any other female versions of the windstorms.

She was a strong wind-teller. Yes, not in a thesaurus, I know.

A storyteller would narrate beautiful stories and entertain, you know.

But, a wind-teller embodying strength herself, spreads her empire everywhere.

Wherever she goes, the vacuum gains air and the air becomes the wind.

Though none of the physics law is applied here for none of us to bind.

I tried so hard to make rhymes, but here I go, all I get is a grind.

A whirlpool, people call her, but she never bothers about it.

Yes, she followed Shakespeare's "What's in a name or whatever?"

Nothing in the universe could stop her whatsoever.

The effect she left behind stays forever,

Nobody could forget her ever!

She was happy. Someone wasn't.

The Volcano, Flood and the Thunderstorm met one day.

We should do something about her; the Flood flooded that day.

The Thunderstorm was angry as hell as he told the flood to continue the next day.

Eager and excited to play its part, Volcano asked, 'Is my turn next to next day?'

Both scolded him saying, "You son of a…umm…synonym of lava. Let physics make some sense till today."

She cared about the universe she has been living in; she was unknown to this.

Not fair, she said emotionally when she rested herself on the desert. (Shit, didn't rhyme)

Someone was happy. She wasn't.

So yeah, the Sun asked why she was sad and why was she resting?

Listening to the story, the Sun went mad and punished the 3 of them with a life exile.

Lazy Draught came into effect later bitching, "Why me, you Sun of a… Whose son are you, by the way?"

She wasn't happy. The people weren't.

"See, I told you, nobody likes me anyway, like a flood, it eventually fills the dam though sometimes over the limit, so what? It's the same as you went to the shower, but instead of the sprinkling you get the spank," said Draught to the Sun.

"Alright. Alright. What should I do then?" said the tired Sun.

The Strong Wind, Volcano, Draught, Flood and the Thunderstorm stood in line.

(Which natural phenomenon is remaining?)

And while the Sun was lecturing all…

"Main Samay hoon," said the timeless Time.

It all happens in its own time. Draught settles the flood. Thunderstorm collides with the strong wind. Sun and the Volcano get to the earthly people, and it's a cycle. There's nothing to fight. Wind will slow down but will blow, sun would not be scorching every day, water will not be generous as always and thunderstorms might just fall on the people.

"It's all relative! Guys, Einstein has proved it. So, back off."

Strong wind, along with the world, lived happily forever.

Thank you. During this entire 60 minutes, your blurred image has been in my mind. I wish I was justified. What's the smiley of a heart, for God's sake, this MS Word!

The stage never disappoints Kevin and neither does he disappoint the stage

You must have often heard people say that when you wake up in the morning, try to think about happy things because then your entire day would be a pleasant one. Well, let me tell you that those people don't know anything. So, feel free to tell them to keep their fake optimism to themselves.

For those who don't believe me, allow me to tell you my story of how the day that could have turned out to be the best turned out to be the worst in a matter of 60 minutes.

6:00 a.m. — Like my routine for the past 2 weeks, even today, I went for my morning walk in the park near my place. You must be thinking why am I emphasizing on 2 weeks? Well, the reason is exactly what most of you are thinking: a girl! Since the moment I saw her, something inside me just clicked, and I knew I had to talk to her. With this thought, for the past 2 weeks, I have been trying to gather the courage to do so but unfortunately had no luck so far. However, today, I had decided that I will talk to her no matter what.

6:15 a.m. — I am walking back and forth across the gate from which she enters, in the hope to at least accidentally cross paths and have a word with her. Perhaps, we might just workout together and maybe, in the end, I'll ask her for a cup of coffee as I am one of those who believes a lot can happen over a cup of coffee. Yeah, I know I had everything planned out. Only, the girl in the picture was missing.

6:20 a.m. — Finally, she arrived but to my disappointment, she was with some other girl. However, I noticed that as I was standing nearby, she looked my way and smiled. Maybe it all happened or maybe it didn't. Nonetheless, even the possibility of it happening, gave me the courage to talk to her that day.

6:39 a.m. — I saw her resting on a nearby bench all alone. At that moment, I was like "Hell yeah! Finally this is going to happen." Slowly, I approached the bench and sat near her without demonstrating any signs of my desperation to talk to her.

6:41 a.m. — I finally looked at her and smiled. In return, she smiled and said "Hi". Beaming inside, I replied "Hi". And, after that, one word led to another and gradually, I became more and more confident about her being the love of my life.

7:53 a.m. — Totally engrossed in my dreamland, daydreaming about us on lunch dates and movie nights, professing our deep love for each other; I suddenly heard two heart-wrenching words that I never wanted to hear at that moment. MY BOYFRIEND. After hearing these two words, it was as if I had become deaf for a moment. Let me just tell you all those cheesy scenes that are shown in movies in this situation are real.

Anyway, this was not the totality of my heartbreak. It was just the beginning. For now, only my heart was shattered into pieces but what happened after completely crushed it into a million bits.

7:59 a.m. — While I stood there like a statue, she smiled at someone behind me, then moved to hug the person. Coming to my senses, I slowly turned around and heard her saying, "This is my boyfriend," with a huge smile. After looking at the person, I was once again dumbstruck, and so was her boyfriend. Because it turns out, her boyfriend was my elder brother. At that very moment, my heart was blown into smithereens as I knew now I had no freaking chance to win her.

8:00 a.m. — So, after a few awkward pleasantries, I said my goodbyes and left them.

After the whole fiasco, I at least got to know one thing, apparently my brother and I had the same taste in girls.

The stage and Kevin never ignore each other

Have you ever been to your cousin's wedding? That too a love marriage, which luckily turned into an arranged one, by the mercy of none other than the famous 'Matchmaker Maasi'.

Maasi, just because your son got fortunate in love on Shaadi.com doesn't mean my perfect match is also waiting there just one click away.

I mean does she even realize the difference in the choices of coffee we both prefer to drink!

All our childhood, the common topic of our fights would be the breeds of dog we wanted to pet. When he wanted a Pug, I was fighting for a Doberman.

"She was the perfect one in the list, never like the old ones," said my brother, confidently.

"Was there a blue tick on her name, like the ones on an Instagram profile, to verify her perfection? Or was it destiny, which clicked right? Or is it just the feeling called love, that makes everything and everyone seem perfect enough?"

I knew I wasn't the perfect man a woman would love to be with.

Average looking and high earning, I am a man with a huge collection of video games, rather than porn on my laptop. When it comes to a woman, keeping aside my good looks and my superman print boxer that I wear 4 days a week, they fail to notice the child in me who craves love and acceptance.

But then why am I judged when I look for physical attraction in a woman, specifically the ones with a fair skin tone, perfect curves, sober cleavage and a highly contoured jawline?

What's wrong in wanting to have the most beautiful girl in town, when all these good-looking women are busy hunting for hot hunks around?

"I am Mr Imperfectionist, looking for my Ms Perfectionist," that's my new introduction on Shaadi.com.

12

The Self-Discovery

"Guys, it will be terrific," they cheered together.

"It may be sore, though. And not sure, it is my face, man. What if something goes wrong?" Kevin said, worried and unsure of his decision.

"Trust me. It will look grand." Said Dev.

"You get it done first, then I shall see." Kevin said, feeling a little unsure but took a deep breath in to steady himself. "Okay. I am not changing my mind about this."

"Go, Kevin!" They cheered him on again.

Kevin was excited; his buddies were in full support of him. He wanted to do this, now even more.

"Physical transformation is like a catalyst for mental change and inner wisdom. You shall see." Ansh added.

As the needle ran its artistry gently on his face, it did sting and burn along the way. The music worked as a balm for Kevin, soothing him. It kept a part of his body moving rhythmically. It seemed pure, palpable, and addictive.

"So, does it hurt?" Asked Ansh, concerned.

"It is worth the pain. It is how a rapper's appearance should be. Ain't I rocking it, guys? Simply magnificent." He crooned, pretending to rap.

"True, Kevin." Dev gave him a high five.

"Totally, dude." Ansh added.

"Yes, Kevin, you have gone from a nerdy teen to a refined rapper." Kabir joined in too.

"Hail Kevin!!"

"I needed this transformation, except it is more of a makeover of my soul." Kevin felt elevated. This transformation served as a confidence booster.

Kevin touched the tattoo on his face in remembrance and looked up.

He saw Neena Aunty coming in with her pet poodle, both in twinning attires. It reminded him of their dog Bruno from when they were kids. He was a dark brown Labrador with gorgeous big eyes, always glowing. He was loyal, compassionate, cuddly, cute—everything you would want in a dog. Goes without saying, all loved him. A best friend to them all.

13

The Boy in Me

Kevin recollected the day Bruno saved his life. When he was ten, Kevin went on a family trip with his cousins to the animal jungle sanctuary to look at some exotic animals and birds and have a lovely time. As they entered through the gates, his father started giving them instructions. They were supposed to walk together; no one was to run away alone to roam around; if anyone got lost, they were to meet up at the water fountain at the centre of the place. They listened attentively, nodding their heads, but their mind was elsewhere, too excited and eager to start exploring immediately and look at the variety of animals. Kevin's father also handed each kid a whistle to blow in case of a difficult situation or an emergency. Armed with instructions and a whistle, Kevin left with Bruno while the others raced ahead of him. He just wanted to be with the animals and his dog. He enjoyed being solo sometimes. While he traced along the trail of Zubin, Tina and his cousins, he realised he felt happy.

When he entered the section of serpents, a chill went down his spine. Not that he was scared of snakes in particular but their presence gave him a shudder. As he walked around reading their names, their breed and observed their shining skin inside the glass chamber they were hissing in, he noticed one chamber was empty. He gazed inside curiously to see if the snake was hiding or maybe of a smaller form.

Suddenly, he felt something rub against his foot and he stood petrified. He gathered some courage to peer down and saw what he was certain looked like a thick snakeskin. Kevin stood there in shock while the others had already moved on to the next section. His hands were freezing numb, unable to reach the whistle. Then Bruno barked at the snake loudly, causing it to move away from Kevin's feet and towards him. Bruno tried to bark him out, and by the time help reached them, it was too late. The snake had already bit Bruno, who was now crying in pain. Bruno was in the last few moments of his life. While they all cried, they praised his bravery. Bruno had saved Kevin. It was an unforgettable trip for him as he almost lost his life but also lost his dear friend, Bruno.

This incident had traumatised Kevin. Not knowing how to deal with grief, he locked himself in his room for several days, only going to school and coming out for food, and crying the rest of the days. After a few days, Zubin came into his room and told him to stop acting like a girl. *Boys don't cry like this!* were his exact words.

His statement made no sense to a young Kevin who was simply sad and wanted to cry. But he listened to his big brother and wiped his tears.

Those words left a deep impact on him but it also forced him to think. Whenever he saw his male friends or family members suppress their feelings, hide their tears or shut off their emotions for the fear of being called weak or called a girl, he realised just how terrible the cultural upbringing has been all along. Why is it believed that crying is a feminine concept? Why don't boys or men cry? Boys grow up with this misleading principle that expressing their emotions or lamentation will make them a less masculine. Crying doesn't mean something's wrong with men but suppressing the emotions certainly means that a lot is wrong with society in the standards that seem set for men. The community today forgets crying is entirely human. It is a biological response to an emotional spur. And it has got nothing to do with gender. It made him think: Does crying make one weak, or does it establish you as a stronger person?

Shaking himself out of the painful memories of his beloved dog, Kevin looked around and noticed a few kids playing under the shamiana. When one of the boys fell and started crying, the other kids laughed at him. One even exclaimed, "What a girl! Boys don't cry!" Followed by a chorus of 'don't be weak', 'don't act like a girl'. They were merely four-year-olds. The kids left but made him reflect on the incident.

He recalled when back in college he had an ear infection because of his earring. His mother had surprised him by popping up at midday with an antibiotic. Naturally, he couldn't believe it. First, she bumped into his pals and asked if they knew where he was. Kevin had walked around the corner at that very moment. Surprised and overwhelmed with happiness upon seeing her, he had run towards her and gave her a hug. His mother was busy watching his friends' reactions, who looked at each other, rolling their eyes and poking each other in disapproval of this public display of affection and of certain eeriness on his part. Kevin's mother had immediately said, "Gosh, Kevin, get a hold of yourself! Don't be weak, don't act like a girl." Although he was only acting out his joy in truthfulness, he had been labelled the drama queen. He often wondered why it was so.

His friends joined him after gorging on some food and taking a round of the celebration in progress.

"Kevin, see here, Ansh got a new tattoo just yesterday." Dev said.

"You can say it is in the celebration of your wedding day." Ansh added.

"Hmm, could you show me?" Kevin seemed interested.

"See, it's here, on the muscles." Ansh rolled up his sleeves and bared his tattoo proudly. 'GOT just rocks' inked in a beautiful font graced his skin.

"That's nice. Really. Cooler than mine."

"Yeah. Isn't it a beauty?" Kabir said.

"Just for you, bro." Ansh smiled.

Kevin knew these transformations to his body were a part of Ansh growing and living his life to his terms in a certain way, just like he once did.

14

Good or Bad

One of Kevin's worst days was when he came home freshly inked. Though he felt different and proud, his family was a different matter.

"Kevin, what have you done? Can't you see how unpleasant you look?" his mother had screeched.

"Oh. Where did we go wrong in raising you? We worship our kids, try and make them perfect, be their friend, and this is what we get. If only you could be smarter, talented, sane, and a good kid like our Zubin. Why are you not like Zubin?" She ranted, once again comparing him to Zubin. How could they not see the terrible effects of their harsh words on him?

"You are useless. Maybe not completely. You can always serve as a bad example." She continued, almost as if she had decided to kill every shred of positive feeling Kevin had left.

"Mummy, please." Kevin calmly murmured, never raising his voice.

"What please, Kevin? Your mother is right. Just look at you! Is this what we have taught you, this is how you want to present yourself? Rings and tattoos!" Now it was his father's turn who thundered.

Breathing in and unable to take it anymore, he said, "Yes, Papa, this is it. I am not a kid anymore; I can do whatever I want to myself."

"Such indiscipline! You are not in your right mind now; I will talk to you tomorrow when you feel rational."

"But, Papa…"

"Go to your room. Now, Kevin."

15

The Bro-Code

"So, Kevin. All set, huh?"

"Yes, Ansh."

"Come on, you look so nervous. And why do you seem so dull?" Kabir asked.

"Kevin, our wonderful bro, is finally getting married. We have had such extraordinary times with our group." Dev was feeling nostalgic.

"Yes guys, fantastic memories."

"I still remember the time back when we were in school where I had my first full body biology class. Our first confrontation with the female body system." Dev reminisced.

"Guys, shush!" Kevin looked around him to make sure no one was paying attention to them.

"Yeah, the teacher was so miffed with us that she started shouting at our continuous giggles. Then the time when we pranked the principal, removing the air from his car tires. Although he tried a lot, he couldn't find out who it was." Ansh added.

"Yeah!" Kabir laughed with the others.

"Oh, I cannot forget the time when Dev crashed his father's car." Ansh barked out another laugh.

"Yes. We were so drunk. Uncle was enraged. He kept blackmailing us to name the culprit but no one said a word. Ultimately, he made all of us give him our pocket money to pay for the dent." Kabir said.

"True." Joined Kevin.

"Oh, remember the time Kabir had his first breakup?" Dev asked all of a sudden looking at his friend.

"Yes! Kevin took us to this lavish restaurant to change his grey mood, saying he had the money. We ate and ate like crazy, had so much fun. Then he told us to go outside, that he would pay the bill and come. We waited for a long time. When Kevin didn't turn up, we went inside and what we saw was simply unbelievable. Kevin was washing the kitchen utensils and was apologizing to the restaurant owner for the money that he didn't have now to pay. Very lucky to have this kind of friend." Ansh went back in time and shared the moment they had been together that while back.

"Guys, I love you." Kevin smiled at them, his eyes crinkling at the corners.

"We love you too, Kevin. You are a scarce species indeed." All his friends agreed, hugging him. The strong bond and feeling of friendship filled the room.

16

The Genus

"Oh, Kevin?"

"Yes, Tina?"

"I am happy for you, my dear brother. I have the best brother in the world. You are now moving on to the next significant phase of your life. We both have shared secrets, watched out for one another, and enjoyed some great times. How you have always helped me in challenging conversations with mummy, and I love our understanding. You have taught me so much. You have guided me, supported me any which way, made me laugh every day, and above all, loved me immensely. Always stay the same. Let's continue to play our games and have lots of lovely small moments that bring a smile on our faces. I am proud to have you as my brother, Kevin, and for being a best friend to me."

"My loving Tina," he said and enveloped her in a hug, "I feel the same for you. Don't worry, I will be with you always. Stop making me cry now. Do you want your brother to cry on his wedding day?"

17

The Parallel Genus

"Kevin, my brother. It is delightful to see you getting married today. You have grown up so fast. My little comrade. I recall when we were younger, we were so roguish. The boxing fights, the kite flying, all the pranking and how while watching horror movies, I would joke around with Tina. Make dumb noises and trouble her with frightening things until she got terrified. I always got you and her, didn't I?"

Kevin shoved the intense need to roll his eyes and said, "Yes, Zubin, thank you for having put up such an incredible wedding for me."

"Chill brother. I do love you."

"Hmm."

When Kevin was five and Zubin was eight, the kids were on their way home from school. It had rained heavily that morning and it was muddy everywhere. Kevin's boots got stuck in deep mud and he couldn't move. After unsuccessfully attempting to pull him out, Zubin decided to walk home to get help. Once he left, it started raining again. Kevin waited in the rain for an hour but no one came. He was tired and finally pulled his feet out of the boots and walked home barefoot. When he got home, he found Zubin watching TV. He had forgotten all about him and their mother presumed he was wasting his time somewhere and would be home soon.

18

Just Another Attempt

Kevin took in the atmosphere of happiness around him, feeling strangely proud that for the first time a group of people was happy because of him. Seated under the open sky, he noticed what looked like a nervous young couple, probably speaking to each other for the first time. It brought back memories from the time he had asked a girl out.

★ ★ ★

Kevin's heart thumped rigorously. Impatiently, he waited beside the staircase. Finally after a long wait, she was all alone. He strolled towards her. He felt his feet turning numb. Still, with some leftover courage, he managed to reach her. She was cheeky. The deep kajal in her eyes made her look valiant. She was bossy in her walk. Her hair was always open, rebellious. But she was pretty in her unique way.

"Hi, Anjali." Kevin squeaked.

She turned towards him, the smile on her face disappearing.

Quirking an eyebrow up, she asked, "Yes, Kevin, what is it?"

"Uh. Would you? Can you? I mean, will you…"

"What? Be quick, or I am going."

"Will you go to the college prom with me?" He had done it, he had asked her.

She looked at him, puzzled. Then her smile widened a bit.

Being clueless, he didn't know what to say or do next.

"Thanks, Kevin, see it was great of you to ask me, but you're not really my type. But since you are here, what's your friend's number? Can you give me Kabir's number?"

Kevin was still replaying the line of him not being her type when suddenly he heard his name.

"Kevin?"

"Yes, Mummy?"

"Since you were not paying attention, I am asking you again. Can you share your friend Rakesh's number? I had ordered some items from his store but he is yet to deliver them. I think I will have to remind him; we need them urgently for the ceremony."

"Sure, here it is." He breathed out a sigh as remnants of the memory lingered and he noticed the young couple had disappeared. But his attention was now snagged by white birds and his sister beaming next to them.

"Tina, why the doves?"

"It feels romantic Kevin. Doves represent love and freedom. Enjoy the moment. It is your wedding, after all."

As he gazed upon the beautiful creatures and their sweet chirping, he retracted in time.

19

The Doves

"Where are we going, Kabir?"

"You shall see bro. It won't be just fun but we will also have a chance to earn some bucks."

"Huh?"

"See, it is a poultry race. Stunning fowl. We bid on them and earn if our bid wins. As simple as that!"

"You must be kidding bro." An alarmed Kevin said.

It was real. Many people made the flock run. They used rocks, tiny whips, even electric pods to force them to perform. Kevin's friends saw it as a fun game but he could see the pain in the eyes of the poor capons. Their loneliness, boredom and frustration from being locked in cramped cages was visible. They did not want to perform painful, confusing and demeaning tricks but seemed to have no choice. He found it repulsive.

"How much are you bidding, Kevin? Come on."

"No, I will just watch." He knew he had to do something.

He silently watched the place from where the stock came in. There was a back door to the room for the stock loaded trucks to enter. He reached the door and set all of them free when no one was looking, and they rushed down the road. At the same time, he too made a run for it. The people were confused wondering where the stock went. Soon, he could hear ruckus as people started demanding their money back. The smile on his face stuck there the entire day, refusing to leave.

"I know you are happy, Kevin. It is your wedding day; your smile says it all." Tina said, glad to finally see the happiness on his face though she misunderstood the reason.

"Huh?"

"Yes, yes." She said gazing at the doves.

"Kevin, would you like some cappuccino? You know how to keep yourself steady, right?" Ansh said, sitting next to him.

"No thanks, Ansh, I am fine."

"It is your wedding day bro. It would be best if you were not nervous."

"Don't think coffee would help with that but okay," he said, changing his mind.

"I recollect the last coffee you had with me. Do you remember? The cappuccino, the girl Cheryl, you, me and my girl."

"Yes. How can I forget? The day with a cup of cappuccino, a girl named Cheryl, and me."

20

The Day with a Cappuccino, a Girl Named Cheryl & Me

"Hi, girls!"

"Hey Ansh!"

"Meet my dear friend Kevin."

"Hello!" he smiled.

"Hi Kevin."

"She is my bestie, Cheryl."

"Hey!" Cheryl said.

"So, let's order some coffee guys."

"I will have a cappuccino."

"Same for me."

"Okay girls. Kevin?"

"A cup of lemon tea."

"Okay." Ansh nodded, taking in everybody's order.

"So, Kevin, what do you do?"

"Huh? Oh. "Nothing much. I...I am a performer."

"Oh, so you dance?"

"No."

"Sing?"

"No no… I am a stand-up comedian."

"Okay." Cheryl said, frowning slightly. "I am majoring in fashion. I love and live for the clothes, the shoes and all of them. It's like a whole another world to me."

"Nice."

"Yes, Kevin. Did you know, the first fashion designer was from the year 1826?"

"No, I didn't."

"Yes, in Paris. The heart of fashion. Earlier, many design houses hired artists. Their job was to develop innovative designs for garments. The clients would examine many different patterns. Then they would pick the one they liked best. Consequently, a tradition began of presenting them to customers and then stitching them."

"That's great!"

"Kevin." Ansh interrupted.

"Yes, Ansh?"

"We are just hanging around a bit. Will catch up with you guys in a while. You guys have fun."

"Okay, no problem."

Ansh left but not before whispering in Kevin's ears, *she talks a lot, crazy….*

Kevin didn't find anything wrong with her.

"You know, I have learnt, fashion items come and go, but style stays forever. For us fashion lovers, being unique and fashionable is the most crucial thing in life."

"That's interesting."

She smiled and nodded. Beneath the table, her damp fists crushed the delicate silk of her dress while her kid boots tapped a rapid rhythm. She went on talking about fashion, being an enthusiast. She raised softly curved arms, and a myriad of gold bangles jangled to the rhythm of the mounting beat. Only her brown feline eyes were visible above the sheer red silk draped loosely about her body and across her legs, sipping her coffee slowly, sparking the imagination of her hushed, grey-uninformed audience, which was Kevin.

He listened to her but subconsciously started picturing them together. She was dressing him up. They attended fashion shows. They had a great time. He felt she was the one. Maybe. Was she? Suddenly, he realised her coffee was over.

"Do you want a refill?" He politely offered.

"Umm…no thanks. Oh, look at the time, Kevin. You are a great listener, I must say. I would love to talk to you more. But I have to leave now."

"Sure. Thanks. Let's meet up soon. Let me call Ansh."

"Yes, please. And Kevin, you are indeed a good friend, but I will be honest with you. I don't see you as anything more than that."

"Huh?"

Ansh heard and just smiled, so did his girl, and so did Kevin.

But their smiles were not the same.

It was awkward.

★ ★ ★

"Kevin?"

"Uh. Yes, yes, Tina?"

"My friends are here and want to congratulate you. Come with me."

"Okay."

"Now let me tell you beforehand, don't talk to them much. Don't laugh either. Behave and don't start with any of your performances here, please."

"Okay, Tina. Don't worry; I will behave as you say."

"Thank you."

"See, now, there are four of them. Two are here to check out the guys, the b****es. But it's okay, they are my friends though."

"Hmm."

"One is my best friend, Seema. You know her well."

"Yes."

"And the other is Aliana. She is timid."

"Okay." Kevin was barely paying attention, his mind still miles away, but politely nodded at his sister's words.

21

Introvert or Extrovert?

One Saturday evening, they were chilling out with some other college friends, chatting about almost everything in the world. During the discussion, they came across the topic of introverted and extroverted personalities.

While everyone gave their retort instantly, Kevin began introspecting. What was he?

"How did this happen, Kevin? Have you lost your mind! You are just 17 and you don't even have the permit to drive on the freeways! Did you take our permission before going for a drive?"

"Umm...I...no Papa."

"How did it happen?"

"Uncle, I was with Kevin. When he was driving, the car behind us missed the brakes and ended up bumping into us at a signal. It was not our fault." Ansh said, hoping it would calm Kevin's father.

"Get in! You are grounded for the next two weeks. You are allowed only to step out for college and then back home. If I catch you fooling around again, I will not spare you this time. You have been causing enough problems for us!"

"Look at the kids today. No apology, no remorse, nothing. I have told you this, you have always been lenient with him. Look at my Zubin. He is so enlightened and has never troubled us for anything." Kevin's mother interfered with yet another praise for her beloved son.

"But Aunty, I remember Zubin himself told us about ramming Uncle's car into the big tree outside your home. The accident had cost Uncle a heavy price to repair the damaged vehicle."

"Shush, Ansh, please let's go in."

"Kevin, why didn't you say something to your parents? It bothers me that you never say anything to them. You don't even look them in the eye and tell them how you feel, you simply nod and bear their harsh words. And today it wasn't even our mistake." A frustrated Ansh said, unable to understand his friend.

"It's okay, Ansh."

★ ★ ★

"Kevin, you coming?"

"Uh, yes." Kevin turned towards his mother though he had no idea for what.

"The pandit has some rituals for the groom." Understanding, he nodded.

"Move quickly."

Kevin quietly obeyed.

22

Who Am I?

"Do you know, according to this psychological identity theory, there are four stages of identity progress. At step one, you have no identity. Like a child, you do what was taught by your parents. At step two, you begin expanding your social circle, like in college. You lack authenticity and try to obsess over fitting in, pleasing others all the time. Then at stage three, it hits you as you begin to experience an identity crisis. You begin to question your choices. You try to explore new lifestyles, options, friends or even cultures. It is like a preparation stage to seek what you want to do with your life. Finally, at step four, you have courageously voyaged through your identity crisis and committed yourself. It could be anything, your job, relationship, values or for that matter even your dreams. You now have a clear sense of who you are and what your direction is in life.

"So, guys, I am sure all of us are at that stage now. So, what is it in that for us? I am at my job. I love it. I can work harder and reach miles for it."

"What about you, Dev?"

"Okay, Ansh. What you said was very interesting. Yes, I would say I am more dedicated to my body. My health, fitness and peace of mind matter the most to me. If I am in shape, I can take in the world around me."

"That's nice. Okay, Kabir?" Ansh asked.

"Hmm, for me it is my folks. I cannot imagine my devotion to anything or anyone else except my wife and my kids. You can rightly call me the family man."

"Great. And Kevin? What would you like to say about this?"

He paused, thinking. What was his real identity? Did he know his life's purpose? Family? Woman? Job? What was it that made life meaningful for him? He closed his eyes.

He could feel the darkness. His adrenaline went through the roof. Even in the dark, he could see the fog machine was at work. The pale mist appeared at the centre. He could hear the slight chatter of the crowd. He felt recharged.

As the bright light shone, they called his name. He knew this was it. Going on the stage was never a fear for him but his strength.

"I am Kevin, an artist, a performer, an entertainer."

23

The Direct Hit

"Kevin, it is so nice of your friends to give you a honeymoon package."

"Yes, it is, Tina."

"Look at them dance. Your friends are so funny. All three of them. I must say though, you are fortunate to have such noble friends."

"Yes. I am blessed to have such friends forever." Kevin smiled and thanked his lucky stars but was immediately taken back to a moment when everything didn't seem all that good.

★ ★ ★

"Kevin bro, that was delightful," said Ansh.

His friends had gathered around him after a performance.

"Thank you, guys."

"So, what is your plan ahead?" Kabir questioned.

"Oh. First, a sumptuous dinner, I am super hungry, and then head home. What else!" He smiled broadly, still high on energy post performance.

"No, Kevin, I mean with life. What is your plan in life? Have you thought of working somewhere?" Dev seemed serious.

"No. Why do you ask? I mean, what happened? What is all this?" Kevin looked at his friends, feeling confused.

"Kevin, we all, your friends, feel you need to get sincere about your life. You are twenty-nine." Ansh reminded as if Kevin didn't know that already.

"Guys, you sound weird. You know I am a performer. I love to be on stage and share the humour. I know I am still an amateur, sort of, and still learning but…"

"No, Kevin, we are saying we get it, humour is your thing, but you need to take up a decent job too. Don't you think?" asked Kabir

"How can you say that guys? You know humour is my passion."

"Yes, Kevin, we know. All we are trying to make you understand is do something more with your life. Comedy is just a hobby. Let it be that way." Dev shared his perspective.

"Are you guys listening to yourself? You know how much it means to me. I am good at it; you guys agree too. But, instead of encouraging me to pursue it more and better, you are asking me to keep it as a mere hobby. I thought you guys understood me."

"Kevin, no job, no girl, no family support, you cannot just let your life slide by you, and then you realise you have achieved nothing. We are just helping you save the time wastage of your dear life." Kabir said

"Oh, so this is how you guys see me. Okay, it is clear to me now. I am the loser of your group. A failure. Right."

"Kevin, please don't take us the wrong way. We love you." Ansh tried to reason

"No, you don't. If you were my real friends, you would love me the way I was—goofy, no job, shy, no girl, humour, anything or anyhow."

"Kevin…"

★ ★ ★

"Tina, could you please get the makeup lady to redo my look? I feel I look terrible."

Kevin blinked at the women, feeling lost.

"Okay, Nora Aunty, I will check on her. Just give me a minute."

"Oh, Kevin, you men are so lucky, put on a catchy attire and set your hair. That's it. You are ready for anything. But for us women, it is so challenging! The dress, the makeup, the hair, the shoes, the accessories, the body—everything has to be spot-on."

"Yes, Aunty." Kevin felt awkward again. He always lost his words when it came to such instances.

Kevin's Feats

Kevin + stage = happiness

> *"Dating is fun, isn't it?"*
>
> *At some point, we all have experienced the fun of dating for sure. Be it your first date or your 50th date, the cringe and nervousness that you feel when you meet someone on an official date for the first time is quite obvious.*
>
> *These nervous jitters often prevent us from setting our best impression, ultimately leading to chaos and what not. Hence, here are several don't(s) that you better not even dare to do on your first date.*
>
> *1. Talking about your ex — Irrespective of how much you are missing your ex, or feeling emotional, or need to escape a boring date with the new person, refrain from telling everything about you. You are just NOT supposed to puke everything about your ex or your past relationships. The date should wholly and solely belong to you and your date.*
>
> *2. Talking about the future — Okay relax! You have met him/her for the first time, and you need to calm down. It is okay to daydream about your future with your date but do not intimidate the person by telling them how seriously involved you are. Your feelings might be genuine but take it slow, give your date the time to settle their thoughts too.*

3. Get drunk — Each one of us is aware of our own drinking capacity, and yet sometimes, we tend to lose control. Boozing on the date within your limits is a great way to loosen up a bit. But hey! Who is going to like someone who is drunk beyond measure? This is certainly a good idea if your bright idea is to spoil the date and bid farewell to your date forever.

4. Become a victim — Perhaps you are facing all the difficulties of the world, and it is a heart-wrecking situation for you, but that doesn't mean you will bore the hell out of your present date. We all go through certain downfalls in life and everybody is not interested in listening to it. Rather, you can take it slow by patiently waiting for your partner to get into that comfort zone.

5. Show punctuality — Be on time always. Coming on time sets a good impression. If you have an ingrained habit of coming late, then start getting ready earlier and leave early to avoid the delay caused by unforeseen incidents like traffic.

6. Tireless attempts to impress — You must relax first. Be confident and do not overdo things at all. If you wish to compliment your date, do it subtly. Keep the manners up and show you care, but do not do things that would make you appear desperate. There is a thin line between being excited and desperate; make sure you never cross that line!

Meeting and dating someone for the first time can be confusing, but you need to take it slow. Pay attention to your date's body language, carefully listen to what he/she talks about and pay attention to their likes and dislikes. Your aim should not be to impress them but to make that special connection which will help you to win over a second date with them as well.

The stage and Kevin are all smiles, always

Some of us have wondered about the purpose of our lives and some spend years and even decades trying to find it. Most of us, however, don't even think about our role in the grand scheme of things during our so-called 'Struggle for Survival'. From the day of our birth, we see life as a rat race.

The King of Salem from the book 'The Alchemist,' narrates a story wherein the protagonist settles for being a baker (a profession accepted by society) instead of fulfilling his dream of becoming a shepherd and traveling around the world.

Some might wonder why a sane person would take such a risk when he can have a stable profession and a roof over his head. But have you ever wondered whether these individuals are truly happy and satisfied with their stable jobs?

I've seen many people who often judge others on the basis of wrong parameters. I mean how can you determine a fish's efficiency by measuring its skill to climb a tree!

That's unfair, but all thanks to our outdated education system which promotes rote learning, I've seen talented artists end up in boring jobs as they become victims of societal pressure. Leading desperate lives, they bury their dreams and sacrifice their true individuality under the burden of such pressures.

Sometimes, I wonder, is such a life even worth living? What is the ultimate purpose of life?

Some think love and marriage is the purpose of life. But I've seen people who sacrificed their dreams and careers for the sake of their marriage. Is this really what unconditional love is? How can it be unconditional if there are such conditions being imposed in the first place!

After reading 'The Alchemist', I realized true love means supporting the dreams of the person you love, even if it means you might have to make some sacrifices, just like Fatima (a character from the 'The Alchemist') did. She knew her lover will never be happy unless he fulfils his dreams. Thus, one needs to realize that those who genuinely love us want us to be happy.

In a world where most people sacrifice their dreams for the sake of a 'safe job', I feel it's the fear of failure that stands in the way of dreamers. Since childhood, we have been conditioned to view failure as a bad thing. When in reality, it's just a stepping stone towards success. But again, thanks to our outdated education system, generation, present and future have been taught to be ashamed of failure. Alternatively, there have been successful men and women who regard failure as a great teacher. They understand the significance of failure in one's life. Besides, how can someone truly appreciate success without getting a taste of failure!

Likewise, some feel guilty about doing what they love because we were wrongly taught to associate work with struggle and what brings joy with guilt. To many, a regular job doesn't bring happiness. So when you find happiness in what you dreamt to do, the feeling of guilt might just ruin it.

When we look around, we see people who have failed to fulfil their dreams and feel guilty about it. One must not forget the suffering and hardships they had to endure to fulfil their dreams. Giving up on what you've dreamt and struggled for might sound saintly, but it is the exact opposite.

So, if you were to ask me what the purpose of life is, I would say it is to live the life of your dreams. Simple! If your life is your message, show the world how it feels to live the life of your dreams.

I might sound a bit selfish, but what is the purpose of living a life without doing something that brings meaning and joy to your life?

There are no accidents between Kevin and the stage

I looked at the crowd. There were over a hundred people out there, crammed around high tables in an underground pub. The host introduced me. Every eye in the room burned into me. I picked up the mic. I could see the crowd laughing away and clapping, enjoying themselves.

I have been a fan of humour since a long time. Back from the daily soap in the 2000s, I have always watched, admired and imitated Paresh Rawal, Rajpal Yadav and Govinda. Over time, I evolved. Presently, whenever I get a chance to troll people (male mostly), I mimic Sheldon Cooper and Chandler Bing.

Laughter is good for your health. What a cliche! Even sex is good for releasing stress. Anyway, I am sitting on the balcony seat to watch a stand-up comedian, Jeeveshu. Waiting for the show to start, let me tell you, I am accompanied by a handsome guy. Lights aren't turned off yet, probably that guy like me is fulfilling his lust by watching the hottest girls of the city.

Some passed by, a few passed beside, while some sat behind. Then, this group of four came. Oh, Charlie's Angels. The Gods must have taken long summer holidays to create these dolls. It wasn't the first time I had imagined Gods on a vacation but sometimes it's winter and perhaps paid leave.

When there is a group of beautiful girls, you have to be accurate about the girl you want to focus on. I selected the least beautiful of them. Of course, I had my front camera to ensure I didn't look uglier than I was!

The girls sat diagonally right behind us. The show started. I laughed and looked back. I pitied myself while my friend tagged me as desperate which I was since ages.

I held myself from looking behind, but then as the show progressed, a cute and most melodious laugh began to enter my eardrums. I had to see who she was.

After all, she was my imaginary wife.

I smiled like it was my last as she was a beautiful lass,

Just looking at her, my life would pass.

Her dark complexion made me secure about my choice,

The curves of her body were silently making noise.

The girl of my dreams, she was the one.

Who wouldn't love the way she did her bun?

Statistically it was unlikely that I would think about a girl for so long because eventually, I knew I would end up just looking at her.

The show ended. We moved. They walked. I watched her with my crazy eyes. She was perfect for me. I looked at myself and I paused. It took me 3 seconds to decide to turn back and let it go, thinking, "She is out of my league."

So, what was I? Introvert or Extrovert? Well, I felt like a performer. However, being a performer is a big deal. Performing on stage was a different experience. It was not the same as socializing. It did not ask for quick responses or even any word recall. Performance never questions, "Why are you like this?" or "Why can't you be like that?" The reward of performance was intrinsic, not extrinsic. Performers love to hear applause at the end and hope their performance was good for the audience. But a big part of the reward is the artistic satisfaction of having accomplished something creative. It's not about any social approval.

Perhaps, I am an introvert who would genuinely love to be in the limelight.

Kevin is the performer of the stage

Rahul: "Did you watch the new episode of Koffee with Karan?"

Riya: "Oh, yes. I love the show. I wish I could be there as a participant."

Rahul: "Come to my house. My Aunt would ask you so many questions, you'll have your Rapid Fire debut right there."

Riya: "Haha. And I can play that embarrassing story a bit in my house since my mom and dad don't seem to stop."

Rahul: "The amount of time Karan spends on asking Deepika when she is getting married seems more than his use of the word 'conjecture'."

Riya: "Oh, the same old question of marriage. Did you see the promotion of Google home in the episodes? Only if Google could help some celebrities to shut up."

Rahul: "The quiz segment looks like me on the weekend, calling all my friends waiting for them to pick up and feeling like an absolute loser when they don't."

Riya: "Haha that's me too. The buzzer round is me trying to live my life looking like I know things and getting people's attention, but when it's actually my turn to perform, I realise I don't know shit."

Rahul: "Haha, see? You are already living the show."

Riya: *"Is that the reason my life seems so trash?"*

Rahul: *"But it is filled with glamour. Wanna watch the new episode together?"*

Riya: *"Does Karan Johar love to show off his shoes? Absolutely. Let's go."*

Kevin and the stage are growing together

Some people are smart as despite their general dislike for children, on occasions such as weddings, they grab a child randomly and play with them as if it were a dream of theirs to have children of their own someday.

Well, that's not the case because for them it's an escape plan. They don't want to get stuck in conversations with anyone. So, let's say if anyone goes to them and says 'Hi'. They would pretend as if that person is saying 'Hello' to the child and not them. So, they would take on a childish voice and say, "Hello, how are you, Uncle? You have gained some weight. You look like an elephant," while the child looks on in confusion.

The conversation would go on while the child would be like, "Utar mujhe, tu niche uttar mujhe. Though I am 11 months old, I feel like I will speak better than you."

But one day, I found something amazing. I saw two random guys holding two random children, trying to find an escape route. The conversation was hilarious as both were insulting each other.

One day out of nowhere I was thinking, "What would happen if instead of women, men went to sasural?" Like just imagine the situation reversal. Here's probably how conversations would go. The husbands: "Suno, me mayke jake au?"

The wife would reply, "Abhi abhi to gaye the 2 saal pehle, kya hai wahaan?"

The campaigns instead of 'me too' would be 'Men too'. Men will be men, will become Women will be women.

The stage gets who is Kevin in and out

Once upon a time in the dark world, there was a devil called Sadick. He was red and scary. People of different colours were afraid of him. He was the ruler. He was a nasty bastard. He was selfish. He was the stereotypical villain.

Then, one bright day in the dark world, a happy face called Laughuck entered and changed everything. He was blue, and he started making friends. Over time he even started making people happy.

This made Sadick angry.

It was #Laughuck vs #Sadick. Who will win? People were tensed. They just wanted a new ruler, and it was Laughuck. But there was no way to conquer Sadick.

Laughuck came up with an idea. He made people laugh out so fucking loud that they turned blue and gathered his army. He defeated scary red ass Sadick.

Laughuck won the battle with just fucking laughter.

#tinytales #shortstory #tinytale

I was being so nontechnical. Let's be some science student.

Laughter decreases stress hormones, increases immune cells and infection-fighting antibodies. Thus, it improves your resistance to diseases. Laughter triggers the release of endorphins, the body's natural feel-good chemicals. Endorphins promote an overall sense of well-being and can even temporarily relieve pain.

Now that I've explained it so well, I'm waiting to hear: "Kevin, you rule!"

The stage is shared by all

"Please give it up for Sid, your laugh riot begins..."

(Audience clapping)

I am going to talk about millennial couples today. Couples these days are so independent. It is the millennial generation. They seem educated. They workout. They are socially active. They are tech-savvy. They seem to know everything. All powerful traits. Except none would know how to enter the kitchen and cook some food. Yes, there is love between the couples, it's all good, but from where will the food come? How will the hunger be solved? Couples today can do any household task by the click of a button on their phone. But they have no clue as to how to do it physically. Like today, if you go see a girl for an arranged marriage, you will see her beauty and financial stability. But that's all.

For you, it fulfils your criteria. But it does not fulfil the criteria for your mother as she does not belong to this generation. For her, it is a pinching necessity to ask the girl, "Do you know how to cook?" And her response would be, "Yes, see here I can order it flawlessly, right now!" Her phone ready with the app open, the perfect menu, and even coupon details prepared for discount options.

For millennial couples, cleaning or cooking or even buying vegetables becomes a glorious task. They get thrilled if they get one-kilo tomatoes for three hundred. They feel great, oh you know we bargained and got them down from a high cost of four hundred. They feel a sense of accomplishment, without a clue that tomatoes cost only fifty rupees per kilo. This is the mind-set of today's millennial couples.

I hope you are having fun.

Also, people today are 'Exaggeration Kings'. Have you opened a LinkedIn or Instagram bio? Every profile is flooded with superficial adjectives.

Hustler, Entrepreneur, Solo Traveller, Owner of my Own Life, No Boss Life, Self-Surviving, Author of my Destiny, Motivator to Family and Friends, Purposeful Human, Homo Sapien and Homosexual—sorry, but the last one was not an exaggeration, it was the truth!

It's sad that sometimes people who genuinely write their bio feel depressed because people still judge them. So I worked as a creative content writer with a company. And whenever someone asked me my designation, I would honestly reply, "Creative content writer," to which they will be like, "Huh, okay, then content writer bolo na. Creative kya?"

I tried explaining that both are different. He wouldn't believe me and alag hi denial me chala gaya. Moreover, he would start explaining to me that I was adding "Creative" as an adjective which is not required.

He said, "It's equivalent to me being a software developer telling my designation as an 'Amazing' Software developer!"

Maine company walo ko bol diya fir "Creative" nikal do meri designation se. Toh company walo ne mujhe company se nikal diya…

"Thank you all for being such a great audience. Adios for now."

(Audience cheering)

24

The Decisive Strike

"Kevin, is this the time to come home? Where were you? Couldn't you call and inform me?"

"I was at an expo, Mummy, with all the hotshots present. I wanted to see the performances. Especially the stand-up comedians. It was amazing! Oh, the place was loud and filled with people; I tried but could not call."

"Yes, you have lost it completely. Going out till late nights and roaming around like this, like a hippie, will not help you progress in your life."

"Mummy, please."

"Why can't you be normal, Kevin? Learn something from Zubin. Look at him. So well cultured and takes such good care of the family. I don't know what went wrong with you. My one child is a saint while another is a devil."

"Mummy, what have I done? Just going out makes me a devil? It is always the same with you. About everything: What I do. What clothes I wear. What time I come home. How many phones do I use? Why am I single? I don't know when this will stop. Why can't you just talk to me once? What do I want? And every time it is about how good Zubin is!"

"Did you see how your son spoke to me?" She spun to face his father, finger pointed at Kevin.

"Papa, I was trying to explain to Mummy…"

"I heard you, mister. You know you cannot talk back to your elders in this house. Not under my roof!"

"Okay, so I shall leave. Leave this hell you call home."

"Kevin. You cannot talk this way!" His father's face grew red.

"But Papa, why is it always this way? Why don't you guys understand me? I have to keep all my emotions to myself, as I cannot open up to you guys. I am not a kid anymore. Please stop treating me like one."

"Kevin."

"Yes, I know. I will go to my room and preferably stay in there forever."

Powerful emotions ran through him—a lot of self-questioning and a range of issues hovering in his mind. He needed to feel alive. He felt worthless. This expressive exposure of dispute, this quarrel, had urged his mind to demand recognition of the self. His parents could be happy with their other two very privileged children. Kevin had no problem with boundaries to begin with and this moment of freedom had been overwhelming but little did he know it would just end in chaos for him. As the night progressed and the moon shone into his room, he recalled the day he'd had.

"Guys, we are going to the expo. It will be awesome."

"Yes, Ansh. It will be great. Can't wait to see all the shows."

"Okay. We will also catch up with our girls at the expo." Said Ansh.

"Guys? I thought it was a boys night only."

"Yes, Kevin, but you need to understand we could not say no to our girls. I guess you won't unless you have one." Ansh shrugged.

All except Kevin had chuckled.

"Sorry, Kevin. Don't worry, we will have lots of fun tonight, and my girl is bringing a friend too. We will help you mingle with her." Ansh added.

"We always think of you too, bro… Now let's go watch the performance by Sid." Dev chipped in.

Kevin felt a little lonely even in the crowd and among his friends.

"So, Ansh, that was a great act by Sid. So, impressive. I am just waiting to see what is coming next."

Kevin tried to avoid looking directly at her. She was standing behind Ansh and he didn't want to look too anxious. She had a charming smile with her eyes crinkling up a little. Her hair looked flawless. She looked gentle and poised.

"Hello, Kevin."

"Uh. Yes hi," he replied shyly.

"I am Ayesha."

"Hello, I am Kevin."

"Yes, I know." She giggled.

The next two hours felt like a dream. They talked, they even danced. She was hilarious and Kevin was elated. They sipped on some liquor too, having a lot of fun with each other. He even held her gorgeous hair back as she puked on the side of the wall. Even the shabby dirt or the smell of the puke couldn't bug him. She was all he looked at.

Her splendid smile, the wonderful time. Kevin immersed himself in this belief that he had finally made it with a girl. While she washed her face, he went on to daydream about their wedding plans, number of children, which school they would go to and the future ahead.

"Thank you, Kevin. I apologise you had to see this."

"No, it's okay."

"That is sweet. Let's go back in."

While he was busy getting some juice for her to feel better, he saw her talking to a guy. Tall, sturdy, smart with a six-pack frame. He quickly grabbed the glass of juice and went to check what was going on.

"Ayesha, I said I was sorry. I realise my mistake now. I promise it will never happen again. I sincerely do!" He heard the guy speak.

"Oh, Kevin, meet John."

"Hi, John."

"Ayesha, please." John muttered.

"Okay, John, you promise? I am giving you one last chance."

"Thank you, sweetheart. You are the best." Turning to him, John said, "Thank you, Kevin bro, you made my life."

"What? Huh. Ayesha?"

"Thank you, Kevin. I had decided to tell you this, but I wanted it to look genuine. John is my boyfriend and we have been in a relationship for the past three years now. He has been feeling a little doubtful about me lately. All I wanted to do was to make him jealous, make him feel how much he wanted me in his life. And that's why I coupled with you for some time. He missed me. Goal accomplished. Okay, see you."

Kevin felt mortified. He just stood there with a glass of juice for a while, not knowing where to go or what to do. He felt so humiliated. It seemed the gravest day of his life. Who would do such a thing and not even apologise? Just manipulating and exiting off.

He tried to recollect the excellent time spent that day, the shows, the humour. But all he could recall was the moment when he stood there, alone and embarrassed.

Back in his room, he had made up his mind. He had to do this.

"Congratulations to you, Kevin."

"Yes, thank you, Milind Uncle."

"Oh, hello, Tina, how are you?" Milind Uncle smiled when he spotted her.

"Hey, Milind Uncle, how was your last trip? To…uh… Where had you been to? It is challenging to remember, Uncle, you travel so much!" She said, rolling her eyes.

He barked out a laugh. "Not to travel my darling, to explore. I love to discover new places, meet new people and take in the diverse cultures of the world in me. Life is short and the world is vast. And yes, I had been to Malana in Himachal. It is like paradise, situated near Kullu valley, with ancient village legacies, muscular ethnicity and marvellous forests. I had a fabulous time."

"That is nice. Kevin has also been to Himachal, some time ago. Where did you go, Kevin?"

"Kasol. It is pretty close to Malana." Kevin felt happy remembering the time.

25

The Journey

"Kevin, are you sure you want to go?"

"Yes, Papa. I need this time. For myself. For some peace."

"Peace? Are you saying we have made your life chaotic?"

"No, Mummy, I did not mean that. I want a break."

"Break from what?"

"Mummy, please." Kevin pleaded.

"Okay, Kevin. I will give you this break, as you say. You have to come back and get serious with your life—a proper job and marriage. You will have to take responsibility."

"Okay, Papa. We will see. Let me go, please."

Kevin's train left the station and a sense of restlessness filled inside him. But he wanted this. He had seen all the falls and it was time he let go. He had no girl, no goal, no meaning to his existence. As it is, life was pointless, and everyone dies someday. He just knew He had to leave, leave to be away from his dilemmas, depart to be in solace. A friend had told him that Himachal Pradesh was the place to be. It was a space of calmness and content. It was ideal for a solo traveller like him. So, he would try it.

The bogie was full. A couple and two children were his companions for the night, and he was glad to have the top berth. He would hide away throughout the journey and have a slow time. He tried falling asleep but couldn't. His companions didn't feel the need to check on him, no one cared if he was alive or not. He felt as if no one cared for anyone anymore. Maybe he should be the same. He got down and went to use the restroom. Someone was in there so he stood by the train door, looking out, staring in the dark. When he heard, "Isn't it getting dense, the cold?" and turned.

"Hi, I am Ryan." He was dressed in a denim shirt and jeans with the top button loose and collar flying behind his neck. His brown eyes seemingly gazed at Kevin's soul directly while the smoke from his lit cigarette whooshed away in his wavy black hair. He looked like the Indian version of a Greek God.

"Kevin." He replied, shaking himself out of his thoughts.

"Would you like one?" Ryan indicated his hand which held a cigarette between two fingers, the tip glowing red.

"No thanks, I don't smoke."

"Good. Smoking is a bad habit. I am quitting it." He took in a puff. "So, Kevin, where are you going?"

"Kasol."

Ryan smiled. "That's great. I am going up to Kasol too."

"Maybe we can meet up and hang out." Ryan stubbed out the cigarette with his foot. "I need to use the restroom. So, goodbye, Kevin."

"Uh. Okay." Kevin watched him go, forgetting about his own need to visit the washroom.

Early the next morning, he made it to the inn. He decided to order room service and pack himself in the room with no human contact, having his hours ahead unscripted. He opened the door to collect his order of food sent from the hotel's service and saw a familiar face.

"Hey, Kevin! You are here too. Nice. Can I come inside?"

"Yes. Hello!"

"You can't recollect my name, can you?"

"No, Ryan, I do."

"Awesome. I will not ask you where you are from or what you do. Let's go out and have some adventure. I believe life is a great gift; you are supposed to embrace it, to the fullest. It would be best if you shared the fun with all. And I have a feeling that you need to have some fun. So, come on, get ready and do get your backpack. I will not say anything more. Meet me in the hallway in 10 minutes. Ciao!"

Should I go? I should dig back in my bed and maybe watch some TV. I'm not going.

"Hey, Ryan!" Kevin said, meeting him ten minutes later.

"Thanks for coming, Kevin. It will be a fun trip. Trust me. I am a terrific companion, that's what everyone tells me."

"Hmm." Kevin smiled.

"We will visit the Parvati River, have a trek to Kheer Ganga and will have authentic Italian food. I do hope you are a fan of Italian cuisine."

After having a fantastic trek, he spent the night taking in a breathtaking view with Ryan and this group of such varied humans. No one knew where one came from or what they did. They were in awe of the site, its simplicity, sharing their vivid encounters, getting lost in the culture of the city. This small town was like paradise with a picturesque landscape that would leave you in wonderment. Everyone else was travelling solo too, seeking remote connections, far away from their everyday life, free from their troubles and creating experiences so unique that would stay with them forever. The 'no internet' and 'no one known period' seemed larger than a life event.

Hearing about the old myths from the locals, reciting ancient lore with them, grasping the prominent tales of wisdom made them explore their multicultural roots. It made them dwell deep and gain insights into different traditions and values followed. Kevin was having the time of his life. Carefree and divine. A time of calmness, peace, solitude along with a reflection of the self. The 30-day long trip made him realize that the purpose of life was to be happy, as advised by the noble Dalai Lama. Sitting on the banks of the Parvati River, he sank into his soul.

Having been lost in time all this while, a feeling of mindfulness ran through him. The trip was at its end. Was he prepared to return? Could he face others? Did he know the answer to the final question?

Who was I?

★ ★ ★

Kevin felt someone tap on his shoulder.

"Kevin…"

"Y-yes, Uncle?"

"I will see you in a while. Let me meet others."

"Yes, Milind Uncle, of course." He nodded repeatedly, watching him go.

26

The New Wave

"Yes, Papa. I have signed the contract. It is a full-time career, and it pays well too. It is what I love doing the most, and I feel fortunate to have found my passion in my work. Very few get such an opportunity, truly."

"That is nice, Kevin. Good to see you display maturity. Do invite us to your next act. We would love to see you perform on stage, all of us."

Suddenly, Ryan's words rang clearly in his mind:

"Keep in mind, Kevin, you are always responsible for your actions and never for others. By understanding this and refusing to take anything too personally, you will save yourself from getting hurt by unpleasant events. If you have such a mindset, you can never feel rejected or ridiculed. You can say yes or no, whatever your heart chooses, without any guilt or any self-judgement. If you follow your heart, no negativity will ever affect you, and you can attain peace, happiness or bliss without the fear of getting hurt. I know, I sound too dense for now. But hold on to the golden words of lord Ryan, thy master."

"Thank you, lord Ryan."

"Kevin…" His father said impatiently.

"Yes, Papa. I will book the seats for the next show."

"Kevin, trust me. I believe a human does have the power to change your day, your mood even yourself. But you also can change larger things like your surroundings, your life's path or even the people you associate with on your way. If you don't like something in your life, you can change it. Most of life's things are temporary, if you want them to be. If today turns out to be a bad day, you have the power in you to do something that changes your wave. Your mood. Every individual can make things the way they want to be. You can change the person you are. The power is yours. Go, Kevin. Walk on the path with your Master Ryan."

"Stop it, dude."

27

In the World of Acceptance

"Kevin, it is your wedding day. Why are you so lost?"

"Hmm? No, nothing, Zubin, I am fine."

"Oh, I remember my wedding like it happened yesterday. It was grand. I was a part of every single affair that happened that day. You recall how the ghodi was so vigorous, I had to tame it to get on board. It tried to kick me even then I…"

There it was, Zubin the great, always making everything about him. Kevin tuned him out.

"Kevin bro. Meet Isha. My wife's good friend." Introduced Dev.

"Hello."

"You were stunning up there, Kevin."

"Was I? I am glad you liked my performance. Would you like to grab some coffee while I share some more of my act with you?" Kevin asked, without missing a beat or stammering.

"Yes. I would love to."

"So, what do you do Isha?" He smiled, holding her gaze.

"I work as a human resource representative at…"

"Look at Kevin go. He has become a pro." Said Ansh.

"Yes, Kevin, when it comes to rejection of love, never fear it. You must be bold as well as prepared. It is always on how you handle rejection, define your mistakes and learn from your failure. Keep practising, and you will become unstoppable, my partisan Kevin."

"Kevin, just a few minutes left of your bachelorhood. Are you ready?" asked Kabir.

Was I? Kevin thought.

As he waited for the final moment to come, the past few months of his life flashed in his mind. It was all that he wanted in life. He was sure and smiled at the thought.

28

The Unlike Me

"Splendid movie guys."

"Yes totally. Boys night out rocks!"

"Let's order up guys. The popcorn was good, but I am still hungry."

"Yes, Mr Potato Head Ansh. Let's order."

"Stop it, Dev."

"Kevin, would you have the burger?"

"Uh. Yes, I will."

"You seem adrift?" asked Kabir. "Are you checking out Grindr?" He asked peeking at his phone.

"Yes. I am looking for a friend I met a couple of days ago."

"On Grindr?"

"Yes. Do you mind?"

Kevin now seemed more confident, he knew what he wanted and didn't let anyone bother him.

29

The Pre-Wedding Epoch

"Will you marry me?" Kevin asked when they were done with dinner and were waiting for the desert to be served. He felt happy, nervous, numb—all at the same time.

"Kevin?" Ryan looked at him wide-eyed.

"I had the best time of my life in those thirty days I spent with you. You made me laugh; you made me confident, I could even flirt, can you believe it? Me? You, Ryan, only you, helped me evolve. I don't care what the world will say or do. I know I love you and want to spend the rest of my life with you."

"Are you sure, Kevin?"

"Yes, with all my heart."

Ryan gave him a wide smile. "Yes, Kevin. I will marry you. I love you too."

"Kevin, are you in your right mind?" Had they been at home, his father's voice would've been a lot louder. Kevin, however, didn't care.

"Yes, Papa, I am gay. And I want to marry him." Kevin wished and prayed they would accept and welcome Ryan into the family.

"Your concern was I get settled in life, a decent job and a future. I am going to have it all."

"Kevin, I feel giddy… My son… I should have expected something like this from you."

"Mummy, it is my life and I get to decide what to do or whom to choose as my life partner. No one can change that." He tried to reign in some patience.

"It is going to happen; I wish you all will accept me the way I am. Family is supposed to be a person's support, for all choices taken, for love, for happiness and for life. I know it is going to be a challenging phase for you to accept this colossal truth of your son's life. But I will continue to love you and will always be your son irrespective of my choices. Only with your support, I can nurture a healthy life. It is very natural.

"I know homosexuality is still not an easy choice in India owing to fear of rejection in the rigid traditional society. But many parents are changing the situation. It is a little challenging to accept, but it is not impossible." Kevin tried to make the situation easy and understand where his parents were coming from but in his heart he knew it was a daunting task.

30

The Unproposed Guy!

I am getting married today. My life is about to change. I am embarking on this new journey of love and marriage. As Ryan stepped inside the pandal, I looked back at my life. How was I? What had I become? My passion for stand-up comedy. I looked at Ryan, and he smiled at me. The hot day, the spotlight of photographers, the music, the guests, everything was a blur for the moment. I could only feel Ryan's smile, making my face smile in chorus.

We took our vows, and I was ecstatic. My family, friends and all the guests cheered and politely ignored the tension of being at a unique wedding. It was amazingly blissful. Each of us believes deep in our hearts in a sort of 'happily ever after' ending. For me this day symbolized the beginning of that perfect life ahead—my happy ending.

I was no longer The Unproposed Guy. Well, I never was!

Kevin's Feats

Kevin and the stage are one – Part I

Written approximately a year before the wedding.

A recall to the unfamous me.

I will keep writing this until I become famous (You can laugh OUT loud).

So, I was at Project Café, alone (do you doubt?) and happy (you wish). I could see two couples but did eavesdrop on one of them. Although I regretted it later. It was usual and fun; they both enjoyed and had a great time, I assumed, and would definitely move on to the next date, only if I could confirm.

The other duo, like always and like every other day, were embarrassing me because the girl was so beautiful and I couldn't figure out a way to find a single reason if the boy was nearly intellectual or smart or (nahi, handsome to tha) aur ha (Paisewala bhi tha). Okay, where was I? 'Why was the girl with that guy?' Are haan, paise ka bol dia na mene? Acha chalo, next.

The girls sometimes look so beautiful to me that I don't even feel like I am human, I am just a pet dog, a real pet dog, who wants to ride the car but would always be in the lap of the side seater.

Kevin and the stage are one – Part II

Once upon a 'Before-millenial' era, an ugly child was born,

Not his fault, the whole town was ugly. (Fortunately, a child had no single horn).

Moving to a city made no difference and gave him a beamer,

In fact, his life was less creamer and gradually became dimmer,

Moving to another big city, the decision was lamer.

Jese faltu mein koi fast bowler se ban gaya spinner,

'You can't keep a girl, NO!' Now, he was a role model for every loser.

His life was a lie, lied between 'Aww' and 'Ooo', never to be fitted as a winner.

The Weak Point Dealer aka Douchebag's Dude walked a mile,

Even the name Lame Loader didn't help him to sit on the aisle.

So, in frustration, he checked some old files for a while.

He realized he would never be able to impress another gender,

Thus, start hua ek silsilla, an essay of all blunders,

From all those blunders, he always expected some wonders.

That wonderful day, the 'wonder' happened wonderfully and then, he lived happily. 'Not The End'.

To be continued.

Kevin and the stage balance all their feelings together

"Guys, guys, I am up next."

"Kevin, we are so happy for you."

"Performance is your thing. You were correct. Forgive us for our non-supporting attitude."

"Don't sweat it, my bros. Let's just put it all behind us."

"Hail Kevin!"

I am on the stage, all set, to perform the famous Tandav on the auspicious occasion of International Dance Day, celebrated to rejoice the art called dance.

Known for a very intimidating personality and high sexual appeal, I was that face of the university, which was not only famous inside the campus, but also in hoardings and banners of many famous brands across the nation, as a model.

All traits of mine were women-friendly, but the only thing that a woman could never accept of mine was my passion for classical dance.

Once, I was out on a date with a beautiful girl, who happened to be studying in the neighbouring college. I had been thinking of approaching her for the last 6 months, and whoa!

Here I was sitting with her on a date. Everything was going good, we both were down two drinks, and I had almost proposed to her, when out of excitement, I showed her my dance videos.

And fuck, I almost had a bad trip watching her lose interest in even talking to me and finally leaving the date, long before the expected time making me realize I just missed a chance on getting laid tonight.

That was the first time my passion for dance actually got me rejected by a girl, who definitely happened to be fantasizing about doing me at night.

Before getting on to the stage to perform the Tandav, I had many feelings in my heart. I was pretty sure I would impress a lot of women down there, but shockingly, I got boycotted by males, for God's sake.

"Sone ki asli pehchan sirf ek johri hi kar sakta hai."

I had heard that a long time back but actually believed in it when the next day, on 30th April, a girl came up to me and congratulated me for being blessed with the art of dance.

"I was amazed to see those abs, actually moving to the beats of the tabla so perfectly. You are a charmer."

We gradually grew to be each other's home, in that town full of strangers. It's been 6 months since we got in a relationship, and today I met her friends for the first time.

I got introduced as an engineer who is into hardcore modelling, which is when I realized she was actually turning me into someone she never fell in love with.

"Why? Is it because I am a male and I am supposed to be forming abs, rather than forming mudras or applying gel rather than putting aalta on my palm?

"Or is it all about being more graceful and expressive than half of the female population of our country? Oh wait, did I just get stereotyped for being that beautiful man on stage?"

The stage and Kevin have a new relationship, of confidence, of trust – Part I

Poor: "Did you hear about Isha Ambani's wedding? Oh so extravagant."

Posh: "Oh, yes. I hate this money-mindedness in traditions. He even got Beyonce to perform while Amitabh and Aamir were present as waiters?!"

Poor: "Looked like the after-effects of 'Thugs of Hindustan' to me."

Posh: "Haha, that is true. Someone said they spent an amount close to a royal wedding."

Poor: "S, what? Both of them finance their respective states. Soo…

Posh: "Many weddings have happened this year. The new generation seems to be realizing the benefits of marriage."

Poor: "Or a Sabyasachi lehenga. Who knows? I told Anisha to get off Tinder and start looking for someone to marry, and I might get her a Sabyasachi lehenga for the wedding."

Posh: "With lehengas so expensive, dowry times look simpler. Why do we care? Our daughters would find themselves a decent groom. Richa's new #candid picture got her 200 likes. She's good to go."

> *Poor: "Children these days! In our times a simple picture of the bride was okay to set up a marriage, in today's time you have to stalk her father's sister's daughter's friend to make sure it's a match."*
>
> *Posh: "That's right. And also check if her Instagram feed is aesthetic enough. You know you have to get the angles wrong in order to create 'art' today. Sorry, I have to leave. I am going to attend a cousin's wedding."*
>
> *Poor: "So, tell me?"*
>
> *Posh: "What?"*
>
> *Poor: "How much are they spending on the wedding?"*

The stage and Kevin have a new relationship, of confidence, of trust – Part II

(Closes eyes)

"Again, have the blessing of your Master Ryan's golden words: when you believe what you are doing is essential for you, it will boost your self-confidence to new heights. Any performance has no boundaries. You always have possibilities to improve, express, make mistakes but never lose your faith, your faith in yourself. So, disciple Kevin…"

"Yes, Master Ryan?" Kevin asked chuckling.

"It is time that you express yourself in the style of performance that you want to."

(Opens eyes)

"This show looks good. The people here are from across the globe. Woohoo, nice choice of place, Nivek. I was almost enjoying the show except the lizard interruption part. Yes, fucking lizard. It made chaos and well, guess who I saw? Brad Pitt? Walter White? Hrithik Roshan? Selena Gomez?"

Well, it's almost near to the last name. A girl who looked like Mrs Bieber sitting beside another gorgeous foreigner Well, all foreigners have always looked gorgeous to me. She was 'light' in the beautiful evening. She must be a vivacious being in her living. She was beautiful. The show obviously got diverted for me when I kept looking at her frequently, when she wouldn't know. I could see her smiling, talking & laughing. The show took everyone's heart. I asked myself, "Where's mine?" Ha-ha, it was there.

I could do nothing but observe her. I could have done many things but hey, patience!

The ghat, the wonderful ghat, her and me. I could literally see no people. I still know what it was, but it was splendid and ineffable. I still remember the polite no she said to 'Fryums' selling kids. I was hungry, I bought it. Maybe she will eat gola and she did. Oh no, I have to... Well, you should, go now.

Though I don't take good photos, I took a few. She was into it so she must be a photographer, I guessed. What could have been done instead of guessing except talk to her. I never tried, and I would never ever.

She left (should I go after her?), I didn't feel good (should I?). I had my beer. I had my dinner (yeah, alone). I thought. I thought some more. I regretted it. I slept. I woke up. I packed. I booked the ticket & "No, no, there's still time to go."

Just like everyone else on Earth, I walked on the streets so I could find a rickshaw. And unlike everyone, I didn't get it because, "You are budget-friendly." The rickshaw-wala becomes rude, and you walk away. Not before you walk 5 steps and you see her. Who is she? Her. "Her" or "The Light". I call her light because there is no possibility that I or any passer-by would notice a girl sitting in the rickshaw within a fraction of a second.

"Go fuck yourself" was not the answer of the strange same rickshaw-wala when I asked him to ride behind her. Yes, I followed her, is what I am implying? "Yes, dude, that's…that's… That's not what you usually do. Hey, does this happen usually? NO."

I followed, sorry, we followed. We lost her, we found her, we kept track of her and so we reached. What is the maximum number of heartbeats it can reach? I am sure it reached the same when I saw her again and asked her whether I could sit beside her.

I missed Chester a lot when the lyrics murmured inside me, "I became so numb."

The light is a spectrum. Particle or waveform, as scientists explained, and she was "Light", she had coloured hair.

Remember Chandler and Kathy? Yes, but here, I wasn't Chandler, and she wasn't Kathy. I was like a black hole, and she was light. The two controversial things in the universe. Will it go forward than a 5-mins "Hi-Hello"?

Well, maybe, because she is a nice person; when she said, "What the fuck?" I couldn't understand the figures of speech. Was it meant to be something rude for me, or was it a compliment? Well, it all rests in peace because "Fuck you, last night's destiny" I got to tell her everything in-person and "Thank you, today's destiny" I could forget the regret part of it.

5 Hours Later

She asked me, "What you saw in us meeting that you want to see me again?" and I could have said,

"Us? I saw something in you…"

I no longer thought of questions like before: "Is my life now the best it's ever going to get?" or "What is my purpose in life?" The introspection on whether I have accomplished enough or what's the purpose of my life started circling my mind.

I had a clear and unblemished stance now. I knew what I wanted, where my life was headed from here on.

The stage and Kevin have a new relationship, of confidence, of trust – Part III

The clock was hitting 9 pm that day. Along with my cousin, we were off to look for a shop to buy some plastic cups for the birthday party. I know, you must be thinking, "It's a lockdown, right? So, most of the shops will be closed."

But somehow, we managed to find one shop open.

I was driving my pleasure, my moped, the only pleasure that I have these days. Reaching the spot, I parked and went up to the shop counter to buy things.

Annoyed, my cousin insisted that he won't come as he was busy sorting out an argument with his girlfriend.

On the counter, I saw a groggy looking middle-aged man, half asleep.

"Hello, I need curry cups."

He looked at me for like a minute with his monolids and after a minute of intense silence he said, "Ehhhh."

"I need a cup for curry," I replied.

"Up? Hari? My child, he resides in our hearts," he said, thinking of Hari, a Hindu god.

I thought the guy was messing with me but then he moved, slowly, too slowly, and I thought I was imagining him trying to move his legs but that was reality. He moved close to me, and the moment he stepped into my private space I smelled that fantastic piece of shit, desi daru.

"I need cups, curry cups," I said.

"Oh, now I see, wait a minute." He went back to the place he was sitting in earlier and looked around a few boxes and then came back to me and said, "You need curry cups, right?"

"Yesss! Cups… Curry cups," I shouted at him.

"Hey-hey chill, you should not be shouting this late or else they will wake up," he said with a voice which was lower than my ex's IQ but the way he said it, scared me.

"Who are they?" I asked.

The guy laughed and said, "They, who are sleeping behind you." He scared the shit out of me, I freaked out and turned around immediately.

There was no one behind me. "What the fuck are you talking about?"

He was expressionless which made me breathless and then he said, "Hasn't your mother taught you that trees sleep in the night?"

"Just give me those cups! Or you will sleep right next to them, forever," I said.

"No-no. I don't sleep this early," he replied with utmost innocence.

"Please man! Give me the cups, I need to sleep early and it's getting late," I gave in.

"Oh yes, we do have the cups, wait a minute I will get them." He went back and messed around with some boxes.

After some time he came to me empty-handed and said, "We had those cups, but they are now sold out."

And that was it. I was so pissed that I couldn't even think straight. I pulled down his shutter and left but I could hear his voice from behind and guess what he said?

"Thank you, kid, I was about to close the shop!" And I never lived happily ever after.

The stage and Kevin are always in sync

With her, the lines were blurred.

I can hold her hand, but I can't kiss her cheeks.

She laughed with me.

She cried on my shoulder.

But my tears were not for her to see.

She talked with me all night long.

She called, and I picked.

Even when my heart was racing just by looking at her smile,

She didn't see it.

Image for post.

My eyes said all I wanted, and she looked away.

She was the only constant in my changing life.

Years and years she held me.

Years over the years she tormented me.

I saw her turn her back on me

And her coming back to me.

She clung to me as if I was her lifeline.

But she never said what I was to her.

She smiled at me.

She held my hand,

But she never said what it meant.

I kept waiting.

And years after years she is still here.

Beside me playing with me over and over again.

I am still here to keep.

But I don't know what she is to me.

I want to keep her by my side in any way I can.

So I have her by my side but so far away.

I can see her but can't touch her.

I still make her laugh and see the crinkling of her eyes.

I still spend the night just looking at her when she is sound asleep.

She snores a little with her mouth a little open.

I tell her every night how much she means to me.

But when the sun comes up, I assume the role she assigned to me.

Even though I don't know what that is even after all these years.

Hoping one day, she will stop from her race to some perfect world

And see me as I see her every day.

I keep hoping that one day she will be mine, as I am hers.

One day she will give herself to me, as I gave myself to her.

One day I will be the one to hold her in my arms and not in my dreams.

One day I will touch her face as I make her smile.

She will be mine all body and soul.

And I know she will be all I will need till the end of time.

I stopped time, so I could be with her.

I am still at the same place I was so many years ago with her.

She keeps running and running

And I am still standing waiting for her to come to me.

I ask myself what is more beautiful than her.

The idea of having her

Or is it the love that I am craving for?

Or it is just the idea of love that I want to have.

Maybe I will only find out when I will have her.

Until then I will wait and be whatever she wants me to be.

She says she is gold-hearted.

But to me, over the years I have seen her every aspect.

That I want to tell her that she is more than that.

I have seen her warmth, and I have seen her arctic antique.

How she keeps people at arms-length!

How she doesn't want to be known but yet thrives at the feeling of it!

She thinks no one gets her, but I know she is an open book.

I can read her every emotion, every thought that goes through her brain.

It's all visible on her face.

Over time I realised that I lost myself.

I was so invested in her that I didn't know what I want for myself.

I left myself at that highway where she told me she doesn't want to end things between us.

Things stopped for me from that moment.

Kevin and the stage never change even with changing times

I had just come out of a relationship recently and had moved on with my life which brings me to this incident.

So, talking about moving on, I have been quite active on Tinder these days.

Like every other guy, I have been right swiping every other pretty girl thrown at me by Tinder. You won't believe me as I got lucky and finally managed to get a Sunday date with a girl. A beautiful, good looking, design student from my city who too was moving ahead with her life.

The date kind of went well with an afternoon lunch at Dominos and a dessert stop at Naturals ice-cream.

We were hitting the right notes. For instance both of us had the same choice of food, same liking for things which are sweet and dislike for people who are fake.

I even proposed a second meet which she was sceptical about, the prime reason being her mother always spying on her.

Only Sundays like this, where her mom would go for an afternoon baking class, could be an apt timing for her. So we thought of skipping out the weekdays and decided to meet again on a coming Sunday.

It was late evening, and we were hunting autos on the busy Sunday evening for a ride back home.

She was a bit anxious too as she was already past her returning time. On the other hand, I was trying my luck to take this date one notch up. I tried cozening up to her gradually while she was keeping an eye on the driver's rear-view mirror whose regular glances already had an idea of what we were up to. We were halfway on our trip when she suddenly noticed that a middle-aged fat lady was waving at our auto to stop. "Oh no, it's my mom there!" she shrieked.

Move aside fast, move to the other side, Nivek. My reflexes were quick to their action, and I sort of glued myself to the other end. I thought the auto driver would not stop, but to my dismay he did and before I could speak up her mom had already noticed her daughter who was travelling in the auto.

As the vehicle stopped, I did not get my head up but could see the lady was suspiciously checking me out before she even spoke to her daughter.

"Mom, what a surprise to find you here. I was just heading back home," she said in the sweetest manner possible.

"Is this boy with you, beta?" mom inquired.

She passed me a short glance and nullified all her mom's suspicion with a negative answer. All I could do was look at the rear-view mirror of the driver who was constantly looking at us through the device.

I did not waste my time and thought of getting down from the auto even though my destination was 3 kilometres away.

As I de-boarded that one hell of a ride, I passed both the ladies a small smile and offered the driver the money. "Sir, what about your girlfriend's part of the ride?" the driver bluntly questioned me.

Suddenly I felt all hell had broken loose and ran away from the place not to look back at the auto or never to call her back but only to imagine what the rest of her journey would have been like after I left.

Well, satirically or ironically, if not her, it will be her sister in future.

The stage and Kevin are never in confusion

There's no question that the early stages of a relationship can be confusing. You might constantly wonder what the person you're dating really thinks of you. Your own emotions may be difficult to fully decipher and trying to categorize them as falling in love or as just a passing attraction can be tricky. Perhaps, there will be times where you will begin to question things like is this really happening? Or are you just prone to feeling this way?

Drawing on recent research (focused on heterosexual relationships), here are some questions to help you sort it out:

"Are you suddenly doing new things?"

As people fall in love, they often branch out beyond their normal range of activities. They end up doing everything in favour of their partners. You might find yourself trying new cuisines, watching new shows, or even exploring new activities like running, fishing, or gambling. People who fall in love tend to report growth in the content and diversity of their own self-concepts (Aron, Paris, & Aron, 1995).

"Lately, have you been experiencing stress?"

Falling in love might be the best feeling in the world but do you know, studies link this experience to a scenario where an individual experiences high stress levels due to an increase in cortisol hormone. (Marazziti & Canale, 2004). So if you're anxious, tense, or just plain jittery, it might be a normal response to the strain of repeated social encounters with someone whose impression matters deeply to you.

"Are you highly motivated to be with this person?"

Transitioning from a casual relationship to falling in love may have a chemical underpinning. Evidence shows that dopamine-rich areas of the brain are involved in the beginning stages of love (Fisher, Aron, & Brown, 2005). These areas are considered to be a part of the brain's reward system which tend to function as motivation boosters. Once couples are "in love" for a while, the intensity of these emotions tends to decline. With diffusion, different areas of the brain, potentially more closely linked to attachment start becoming active.

"Does the person you're falling for return your feelings?"

If you're a woman and you feel like you're falling in love, you might be interested to know that women experience reciprocity in those emotions more than men (Sanz Cruces et al., 2015). Maybe women are more capable of holding back their emotions as compared to males, or it may even be a fact that in comparison to males, women are more successful at seducing their partners.

In either case, women who think they're falling in love tend to have their feelings reciprocated more often than men, making them more likely to find their feelings turn into relationships.

"How intense are your emotions?"

People high in attachment anxiety (i.e. they question their own self-worth in relationships) tend to experience a high degree of passion when romance is budding (Sanz Cruces et al., 2015). If that's not you, a lack of intense feeling isn't necessarily a sign that Cupid hasn't struck—not everyone experiences falling in love the same way. In fact, those who have avoidant attachment orientations tend to fall in love with much less intensity.

"Do you fall in love frequently?"

If falling in love is a feeling, you feel it more frequently. You'll have less chance of missing the real thing but more chance of heartache from mistaking attraction for something more. New evidence suggests that men fall in love more frequently than women do (Sanz Cruces, Hawrylak, & Delegido, 2015). Researchers can explain this tendency from an evolutionary perspective, linking love to sex: Thus, women are more likely to be stringent in their partner criteria before declaring love, because their potential investment in an offspring is greater (e.g., pregnancy, childbirth). Such emotions for men might promote reproduction and could therefore be considered evolutionarily advantageous.

"Are you tempted to say 'I love you'?"

A sure sign of romantic interest, some people are more hesitant to utter these three words than others. Although people might imagine that women are the first to utter it, though, research on heterosexual couples again indicates that it's men who are more apt to say "I love you" first (Harrison & Shortall, 2011). They also tend to fall in love faster.

"Are you investing more in this person?"

One hallmark of successful couples is an investment. Be it investing time, energy or emotions; people tend to give it all when they are in relationships (Rusbult, 1980). Additionally, people falling in love are likely to increase their investment in a person by linking their lives together in a way that might promote commitment and stability.

Kevin and the stage get along

Yes, so, what is it about people who have OCD of cleanliness? Well, if you visit their house and move a chair even by an inch, they would be like, "No. It's my house and the chair needs to be right at the place that I want it to be."

Have you ever seen anyone scrub a ceiling, or polish a towel bar? My cousin's mother has hyper OCD; she would clean the TV even when it would be on. Once we were watching a cricket match at my cousin's place. We were excited as the batsman had hit the ball high in the air. We were waiting eagerly to find out whether it was a six or the fielder ends up catching the ball. But alas, all we saw was the squish of colin on the TV screen. You won't believe there have been instances where Aunty would just be ready with her cleaning equipment right when we were having our dinner. A drop of sauce or curry on the dining table and she would rush in to clean it immediately.

Such people are crazy with their cleaning. Even if she would see the neighbour's kid looking shabby, she would immediately call him inside, clean his clothes, comb his hair and then send him off. The parents would wonder if the kid had gone to the garden to play or had he visited some spa?

They have rules for everything. For example, the furniture needs to be placed correctly. Laundry needs to be done regularly. Even if the laundry is expensive, still you need to do it. Why is the giraffe magnet placed after the elephant one, when I had put it correctly? No changing it, please. If the door opens in the morning, she will get a peek of the neighbour's house. If it looks dirty or messy, then you can expect her to start cleaning their house as soon as their door closes. How will she stay across such a home? Even if it is a few steps away! She knows it is there and that fact will continue to haunt her. Their bathrooms always smell nice and clean. They have seven different types of soaps, for cleaning around and maybe eleven additional towels, for members, for guests, for house help and for that matter, even for neighbours. What if they drop in for a surprise visit? They will certainly wish to have their own separate towel.

The children are to always remove their shoes and coats at the entrance before entering the house. Likewise, children are strictly made to change their clothes as that will prevent the house from becoming dirty. No one is allowed to eat in the kitchen because it would create a mess. Instead, one had to eat on snack trays in one corner of their family room and to vacuum the floor immediately afterwards.

A need for symmetry was also part of the whole problem. In the clothes closets, all the hangers had to be at the same distance apart. All boxes, cans, and containers in the pantry and the refrigerator need to be in line with the labels facing forward. The same applied to the medicine cabinet. Every new thing that came into the house such as toys, clothes or groceries had to be washed, wiped or cleaned and then put away in its unique place.

"It's like living in a museum, isn't it?"

Kevin and the stage

Hello beautiful girls and just guys! I just came here to check if I can make at least a single person laugh because no, my roomies don't even giggle at my PJs. This is my first open mic ever. So, yes, I am scared, and there's definitely going to be a shit of load on you, so bear & spare me.

All the Grammar Nazis, kindly ignore your ego to rectify my auxiliary verbs, abstract nouns and any weird adjectives that I tried to fit into the conversation when you aren't laughing. Please.

And needless to say, this work is purely fictional, and I don't want to hurt anyone's feelings, but I may because 'meri feelings bhi hurt hui hain.

I remember the time when I anchored a college function (I shouldn't), I spoke, "Rangeela, mane maro dhol" instead of "Rangelo maro dhol".

What could have possibly struck my mind at that time?

So, it all started when I found my match, not on Tinder, but on a room match. I am his soulmate because he is single and genius. I call him 'G spot'.

It's hard to find him too.

Recently, I was updating my Facebook profile, and he said: Bhai, duniya Reddit pe hai and you are still on FB. I don't use FB blah.

This guy ruined my life with his singleness. The vibes were so strong that he made me single too. I was so happy and content with Facebook, and he advised me to try Twitter.

You know my mother had made a matrimonial resume too.

Engineer. Skills: Facebook Photography. 100 likes guaranteed; speculates a rise of 300 per cent hike if he gets a wife.

Ruined. Verified.

I tried but couldn't even get 3 figure followers on Twitter.

It's so tough to get 'Unpaid' and 'Unpadh' followers, man!

On Facebook, you can write shit; you can write an essay because nobody gives a damn about you in real life.

On Twitter, I felt more lonely and insecure. I can't express myself. So, I would start with (in order to fit in 140 characters), "Girl, I saw you in pink, I blinked, Can we have sex please, please? I will pay return fare too."

The transition was difficult, "Photographer se Writer.

I told my mother to edit my resume too.

Edit: Requires only 140 characters to reach sexting.

Just when I learned Twitter, Facebook found its new love, Instagram.

What the hell? "Ab toh mein writer hun na, Ma? Fir se Photographer ban jau?"

It's such a feminist social network. I failed in that too.

Then my friend said, "Bhai, Snapchat daala, Snapchat daala?" I was furious.

I said, "Out of so many important things to deal with, you always ask me for something I am devoid of. I feel impotent."

I tell you, I can never ever Snapchat. It's a nightmare app. So, I thought I better switch to Orkut, but then before I could, it was already shut down. Now, I only had one option.

"PORN."

Tell me, "What's one of the common things in lick, dick, suck and fuck? It's the CK."

"Calvin Klein."

I saw the quote on one of my virgin friend's mobile covers, "68. You owe me one."

I couldn't resist. Eventually, I told him "Dude, 69 is ulta sex. When was the last time you had seedha sex?"

He said, "I am single, and I need no love."

I was like "Bhai, tu gaali me bhi love boldeta hai. You don't say love, you have always said love-de."

Okay, we are talking about porn, and I must say that it's funny sometimes when there is a foreplay in the foreplay.

The hero, the accountant, the robber, banker, plumber, pizza guy or the president. Anybody except a normal homo sapien finds the toughest way to enter into the house of a hot woman when it comes to porn.

The front door is always open. The lady, for some reason, I don't know, and I wouldn't even try to figure out why, is cooking naked.

Then somehow, after they talk and when he does something, she says, "No, you can't do this to me. It's wrong."

"Okay, wait. So, cooking naked with the door open was right? Let him do his job, you do some blowjob so that I can finish my climax job."

See she is saying, "Na na" and I am feeling like they are bargaining.

It's like the hero said, "Sirf ek kiss and anal, baal bandhlo, bun banalo aur man manalo."

And when she says, "No", I with one hand controlled could just raise the other hand and say, "Give him love, behen ki love-di. He licks, you suck, and that is how you will be fucked."

"PORN = We write it right!"

Were the stage and Kevin ever unproposed – Never

I was reading a book recently. In that story, the book felt disowned and heartbroken.

"It's the same old story, isn't it?"

So, I thought of writing something on it.

Image for post.

HE: "Ok, Google, what is the meaning of unproposed?"

Google: "Unproposed is an antonym of the word 'Proposed'. Here, the definition of the word 'Unproposed' is nothing but every lame guy or girl who has not been blessed with an appealing personality, so they can't or have failed to attract a single person in their life."

Another HE: "Siri, who is an unproposed guy?"

Siri: "Didn't you hear Google, bitch? You and people like you are those who…"

A guy who has not been proposed by the same (lol) or opposite gender. Here, the irony of the word lies in the eccentricity of it. Unproposed doesn't at all mean he is ugly, lame, weak, or dumb. It's just that he has not been in the focus or anywhere near the radius of a girl's retina. A pessimist would say it's all about luck (not me, I am a realist).

List of Kevin's Feats